"I know you
Who is the father?" Kane asked.

Through the doorway, Raoul stared at Julia. Her cheeks had turned white, every trace of color erased. She'd begun to stand, but now slid into her chair as if she didn't have the strength to remain upright.

"W-what?" she whispered.

"You're pregnant. It all adds up. The nausea, the weight gain, the crackers." Kane ticked each detail off on his fingers.

"What are you talking about?" Raoul demanded.

Startled, Kane whipped around. "I didn't know you were there."

"Obviously."

"Who's the father?" Kane asked with quiet insistence. "How far along are you?"

"Almost seven months. The baby is underweight," she said, her vice wobbly.

After a long look at Julia's guilt-filled face, Raoul turned to Kane. "If Julia is seven months pregnant, then she is carrying *my* child."

Dear Reader,

What are your New Year's resolutions? I hope one is to relax and escape life's everyday stresses with our fantasy-filled books! Each month, Silhouette Romance presents six soul-stirring stories about falling in love. So even if you haven't gotten around to your other resolutions (hey, spring cleaning is still months away!), curling up with these dreamy stories should be one that's a pure pleasure to keep.

Could you imagine seducing the boss? Well, that's what the heroine of Julianna Morris's *Last Chance for Baby*, the fourth in the madly popular miniseries HAVING THE BOSS'S BABY did. And that's what starts the fun in Susan Meier's *The Boss's Urgent Proposal*—part of our AN OLDER MAN thematic series—when the boss... finally...shows up on his secretary's doorstep.

Looking for a modern-day fairy tale? Then you'll adore Lilian Darcy's *Finding Her Prince*, the third in her CINDERELLA CONSPIRACY series about three sisters finding true love by the stroke of midnight! And delight in DeAnna Talcott's I-need-a-miracle tale, *The Nanny & Her Scrooge*.

With over one hundred books in print, Marie Ferrarella is still whipping up fun, steamy romances, this time with three adorable bambinos on board in *A Triple Threat to Bachelorhood*. Meanwhile, a single mom's secret baby could lead to Texas-size trouble in Linda Goodnight's *For Her Child...*, a fireworks-filled cowboy romance!

So, a thought just occurred: Is it cheating if one of your New Year's resolutions is pure fun? Hmm...I don't think so. So kick back, relax and enjoy. You deserve it!

Happy reading!

Mary-Theresa Hussey

Mary-Theresa Hussey
Senior Editor

Please address questions and book requests to:
Silhouette Reader Service
U.S.: 3010 Walden Ave., P.O. Box 1325, Buffalo, NY 14269
Canadian: P.O. Box 609, Fort Erie, Ont. L2A 5X3

Last Chance
for Baby

JULIANNA MORRIS

SILHOUETTE *Romance*®

Published by Silhouette Books

America's Publisher of Contemporary Romance

Special thanks and acknowledgment are given
to Julianna Morris for her contribution to the
HAVING THE BOSS'S BABY series.

For my mother—a special lady whose creative talent,
humor and intelligence I will always admire. I love you.

 SILHOUETTE BOOKS

ISBN 0-373-19565-6

LAST CHANCE FOR BABY

Copyright © 2002 by Harlequin Books. S.A.

Visit Silhouette at www.eHarlequin.com

Printed in U.S.A.

JULIANNA MORRIS

has an offbeat sense of humor, which frequently gets her into trouble. She is often accused of being curious about everything…her interests ranging from oceanography and photography to traveling, antiquing, walking on the beach and reading science fiction.

Julianna loves cats of all shapes and sizes, and last year she was adopted by a feline companion named Merlin. Like his namesake, Merlin is an alchemist—she says he can transform the house into a disaster area in nothing flat. And since he shares the premises with a writer, it's interesting to note that he's particularly fond of knocking books on the floor.

Julianna happily reports meeting Mr. Right. Together they are working on a new dream of building a shoreline home in the Great Lakes area.

Note to self: Who's having my baby?

Trudy—hopeless romantic, office gossip, can't keep a secret. *If it's not her, she might know who it is!*

~~Lauren Connor~~—dates a lot, trying out new looks to impress her boss, was out sick with stomach *flu. Hmm...*

~~Sharon Davies~~—recently trapped in an elevator with a major client, blushes whenever he's around, looking a little green lately. *Could she be carrying my baby?*

Leila—makes eyes at me. *Is it more than a crush?*

Maggie Steward—my personal assistant, wants children, clock is ticking. *She would never go to a sperm bank!*

Julia Parker—worries that her endometriosis could make her infertile. No man in her life. *Definite sperm bank material!*

~~Jennifer Martin~~—eight months pregnant. Is it her late fiancé's baby? *Is it mine?*

WHEN THE LIGHTS WENT OUT... October 2001
A PREGNANT PROPOSAL November 2001
THE MAKEOVER TAKEOVER December 2001
LAST CHANCE FOR BABY January 2002
SHE'S HAVING MY BABY! February 2002

KANE HALEY, INC.
Chicago, IL

Prologue

Sperm bank?

Oh, God.

Kane Haley rubbed his two forefingers against his aching temples and wondered for the ten-thousandth time which woman in the company was carrying his child.

He'd never expected this complication. The only reason he'd "deposited" sperm in the first place was to help out a friend, and now it was a disaster. Kane had already expended a fair amount of anger toward the Lakeside Reproductive Clinic for their mistake, but a flicker of irritation rose again at the memory.

We're sorry, Mr. Haley, but we must protect the woman's privacy.

Privacy.

What about *his* privacy? His rights? They'd made him a father with their high-tech medical procedure, and he didn't even know who the mother might be. He had a lawyer working on the issue, but in the meantime, it was driving him crazy, wondering.

Sitting back, Kane thought about the various women working for Kane Haley, Inc…women of childbearing age.

Okay, he knew it wasn't Sharon Waterton, one of the company's accounting assistants. At least, it seemed unlikely considering the way she and his client, Jack Waterton, had hooked up. Other names flitted through his head, such as Jennifer Holder, but the timing of her pregnancy was wrong.

And it was still a toss up whether Lauren Mitchell was even pregnant. A reluctant grin creased Kane's mouth as he thought of the chase she'd led Rafe Mitchell on. His Vice President of Mergers and Acquisitions had found it was a lot more trouble acquiring a wife than anything he'd worked on for Kane Haley, Inc.

So, if it wasn't Sharon or Jennifer or Lauren, who was the mother of his baby?

Groaning, Kane opened the top drawer of his desk and retrieved a bottle of aspirin. He swallowed two and headed for the door of his office. He'd never realized there were so many pregnant women in the world.

And how many of them worked for his company.

Chapter One

Outside Kane's office...

"Are you available this afternoon?"

"For what?" Twenty-seven-year-old Julia Parker smiled at Maggie Steward, administrative assistant to the company's president.

"The new Chief Financial Officer is arriving today. His name is Raoul Oman. You met him at that D.C. conference last June, remember? Kane will be tied up in a meeting and he asked if you would show Mr. Oman around."

Raoul Oman.

Julia stared, the blood draining from her face.

Oh, yes, she'd met Sheik Raoul Oman. The man was permanently engraved in her memory. Instinctively, her hand went to her stomach. The morning sickness she'd suffered from for her entire pregnancy threatened to go out of control, and she took several deep breaths, trying to calm her queasy tummy and racing heart.

Maggie's eyes were compassionate. "I guess you do remember him."

"Y-yes." Julia swallowed and shook her head to clear it. She'd never expected to see Raoul again, and the shock was a bit more than she could absorb—not to mention the embarrassment and a healthy dose of guilt.

"You aren't having trouble with the...uh...?" Maggie's gaze flicked to Julia's rounded stomach, then back to her face. The question didn't need to be finished. The baby was seriously underweight, and so far she'd been able to camouflage her tummy with heavy sweaters, despite being almost seven months along. Most of her co-workers didn't even realize she was pregnant, or else they'd just been polite and not said anything.

"I'm fine," Julia assured quickly.

It was a lie, but she could hardly explain. She gulped again when she saw Kane Haley staring at her from the door of his office. He'd been acting strangely for the past few months, though as president of his Chicago-based company he could act any way he darned well pleased.

"Uh...I'll be happy to show Mr. Oman around," she told Maggie, snatching her hand away from her stomach. She fled to her own office on the 16th floor and sat for several shattered minutes, trying to decide what to do.

Her family plans were getting ready to fly apart, and there was nothing she could do to fix them.

The phone on Julia's desk buzzed, and she gratefully pushed her lunch aside—milk and a package of crackers—and picked up the receiver. "Yes?"

"This is Trudy, in reception. I was told to notify you when Mr. Oman arrived."

Swell.

"Thank you. I'll be right down."

"I'll tell him, Ms. Parker." Trudy sounded star-struck, which wasn't surprising. One look at Sheik Raoul Oman and she must have melted in her chair. The man had sex appeal that could bring the dead back to life.

Julia glanced in a mirror and smoothed her fingers over a stray lock of hair. She didn't care if she looked attractive, just neat and professional. Then, squaring her shoulders, she went to the elevator and punched the Down button. A minute later she stepped out and saw the back of Raoul's dark head.

Flutters hit her midsection even harder, and she gulped down another wave of nausea.

"Sheik Oman," she said, congratulating herself on the cool, even tone of her voice. "Welcome to Kane Haley, Inc."

Raoul turned with catlike grace, one eyebrow lifting. "As you know, *Ms.* Parker, I do not use my title in America."

She knew. She also knew that nothing could make Raoul anything other than what he was—a member of the royal family in his own country of Hasan…and the father of her baby.

It was the father-of-her-baby part driving hordes of butterflies through her system. Or was it the memory of the way he'd made her feel? She hadn't wanted to lose control during their brief, explosive affair, but he hadn't allowed anything but her complete surrender in the bedroom.

Julia's mouth tightened.

The pleasure had been extraordinary, but you couldn't live on pleasure. If anything, he'd proved that a man, particularly from his exalted family background, had trouble letting a woman be equal. Even in the most private of circumstances.

"Mr. Haley is tied up in a meeting this afternoon. He asked me to show you around," she said.

Raoul inclined his head and smiled. "Kane has already explained this matter. I requested that you might take his place."

"Oh."

Any hope that he'd forgotten some of the more *intimate* aspects of their relationship vanished at the dark heat in his eyes. He remembered everything. And he seemed to be reminding her that she was the one who'd chosen to say goodbye. That it was her decision not to prolong the time and passion they'd shared.

But didn't men prefer temporary relationships?

Even men from other countries?

She wasn't the most experienced woman in the world, but from what she'd seen, commitment was the last thing the male animal usually thought about.

"Kane was not aware that we were…acquainted," Raoul murmured. "I thought you might have mentioned me."

From behind his back Julia saw Trudy mouth the words *ohmigod, you know him?* The receptionist looked more excited and dreamy than ever. But then, Trudy was the queen of high drama and romance. She lived for office gossip, though in a kind way. She never repeated anything cruel.

"Kane is the president of the company. We talk about business-related matters," Julia explained, more uncomfortable than ever. "Not about people I've met...at a business conference."

"Ah." The subtle humor lingering in the depths of his brown eyes made her wince, but there wasn't anything she could say in protest. Raoul could communicate more with his eyes than most people did verbally, and right now he was laughing at her attempts to pretend nothing had happened between them.

"Well," she said briskly. "Shall we start?"

"That would be excellent."

She turned on her heel and launched into a description of the three floors of the building leased by the company. She knew Raoul well enough to know he wouldn't need any description of Kane Haley, Inc. He was the sort of man who would have investigated the accounting company from top to bottom before he ever considered taking the position as its Chief Financial Officer.

It almost made her smile. Kane Haley had probably felt as if *he* was being interviewed for the job, rather than the other way around. Of course, the whole thing would have just amused Kane, and it certainly hadn't blinded him to Raoul's exceptional qualifications for the position.

Darn it.

When they were finished touring the fourteenth floor, they stopped in front of the elevators. Raoul had suggested they simply take the stairs, but Julia couldn't reveal that her doctor had recommended no climbing until after the baby was born, so she'd said they were mostly for emergencies.

Normally she didn't babble, but the continuing amused glint in Raoul's expression and the memory of their past relationship was turning her logical brain into mush.

They stepped inside the empty elevator car, and no sooner had the doors closed than Raoul pressed the Hold button.

"Bien-aimée," he said softly. "It has been a long while."

Julia's heart skipped a few beats. "Not so long. Just two or three months," she tossed off, as if she didn't have a clear idea how much time had passed. Fat chance. She had a biological reminder growing in her womb, telling her exactly how long it had been since they'd last seen one another.

"Over six months," he corrected. "June was a beautiful time in your nation's capital."

She kept her gaze glued to the Hold button he was depressing. "We'd better get going, or someone will think the elevator is broken."

"They will simply think the machine is slow."

"Raoul—"

"Julia," he mocked, using her same exasperated tone. "It is good to hear that you remember my first name."

Unaccustomed heat bloomed in her face. "I remember."

"As do I." He lifted his free hand and stroked the curve of her cheek. "I remember many things."

"Please, Raoul. It was nice, but it was just one of those temporary things." Guilt nearly made Julia choke on the words, because, while she had intended things to be temporary between them, she'd deliberately done everything possible to ensure he'd give her a child.

It was my last chance to be a mother.

Julia bit on the inside of her mouth, knowing she

deserved that small stab of pain. Raoul hadn't been her last chance for motherhood, but the longer she'd waited, the smaller her chances would have gotten. Endometriosis didn't always result in infertility, but it was a common result of the condition. She'd gone to the conference still in shock after hearing the bad medical news, and when she'd met Raoul it had seemed like the answer.

"I did not choose for it to be so very temporary. You are the one who made this decision."

Raoul didn't look amused now, but angry, and she could well imagine him as an imperious desert ruler of old. She should have known it would irritate him, not getting to be the one who broke things off. Men liked to be in control, which was why she *didn't* want her child's father involved in their lives.

She'd had enough experience with overbearing, dominating men who thought they ruled the universe just because fate had given them a particular set of chromosomes. Her military father was a case in point. Sure, not all men were like that, but she hadn't had any luck telling who was a control freak and who wasn't.

"We really have to be going," she said. She tried pulling his hand from the button, but he held fast. "Raoul, let go."

"We must talk." Raoul watched the changing expressions in Julia's face and wondered why she had been so adamant about ending their affair at the conclusion of the conference. Even now she fascinated him, stirring his body in a way that made it imperative that he wait before leaving the privacy of the elevator car. It would not be prudent to allow anyone at Kane

Haley, Inc., to see his undisguised response to another employee.

"We have nothing to talk about," Julia snapped.

A flicker of admiration crept through Raoul. At any time Julia was glorious, but angry? Gold flashed from her hair and eyes, color brightened her silken skin and she breathed deeply, emphasizing the womanly part of her that he'd already enjoyed so much. He drew a harsh breath of his own, exerting control over his unruly body.

"Nothing?" he asked. "Perhaps you would like to explain why you gave me an incorrect phone number."

Julia's eyelids dropped, concealing the hazel gold of her eyes. "Did I?"

"You know you did. Although the lady at the dry-cleaning establishment was quite cordial, I did not wish to speak with her, I wished to speak with you."

"You could have called the company and gotten the number."

"Since it was obvious you did not wish to speak with me, I respected your wishes. Now I question if that was the correct decision. You are being very evasive, Julia."

"I told you—"

"Yes," Raoul interrupted impatiently. "You told me many things. Some I have chosen to ignore."

"That's arrogant."

"Isn't that what you expect? The sheik who is as arrogant as his royal Arabian heritage?"

"It's not your royal anything making you arrogant," Julia returned. "It's…" She stopped, clearly feeling she'd already said too much.

"Ah, yes. You do not think well of my sex, I think."

"It isn't necessarily your sex I was thinking about.

In some ways that part is impressive.'' Her gaze flicked downward for a brief moment, and he grew hard again.

She was impudent.

And sweetly naughty.

In the old days of his country a woman such as Julia would have been a disgrace, but no longer. As a youth his grandfather had embraced new ways of thinking about women, and for two generations they had been free to speak their minds in Hasan.

Sometimes that wasn't always a blessing.

''I still do not understand why you wished such a temporary arrangement,'' he said. ''It doesn't seem to be your nature.''

''Of course it is.''

Despite the denial, her gaze shifted once again, this time in evasion, and Raoul sighed.

''You are not promiscuous, *chère.*''

Julia glared. ''Stop calling me…French things.''

He suppressed a smile, demanding control of his mouth. French endearments came naturally to him. Though his grandmother had spent far more years in Hasan than in her homeland, she remained exquisitely French, from the tips of her toes to the top of her perfectly coiffed head. He had spoken her native language from the time he was in his cradle and was named for *Grand-mère*'s own father.

''Julia, the fact remains that you are not the type for such casual encounters.''

''That's ridiculous. You know nothing about me and don't have a clue about my romantic life.''

He smiled knowingly. ''A man knows when a woman has not been intimate for a while. There is a certain hesitation in her body when he—''

''Never mind,'' Julia said hastily, certain her face

was burning from embarrassment. Raoul was too knowledgeable for comfort, and if he was convinced she'd been celibate for a long time he would never believe the baby wasn't his. The question was, what would he do once he figured it out?

Maybe she should tell him first.

Or maybe she should quit her job and leave town.

Oh, right. That's a great solution.

She enjoyed the stability of her position at Kane Haley, Inc., and she was darned good at it. The Assurance and Advisory Service Division where she worked was growing by leaps and bounds. She had an excellent salary, and a number of friends here in Chicago. Leaving was not an option, particularly with a baby on the way.

All at once the demanding arrogance vanished from Raoul's face, and he removed his hand from the control panel. "You are right. People will wonder if we overly delay the elevator."

His expression had closed to the point she would never have guessed they were discussing anything more intimate than the corner deli, and she shook her head. How could a woman hope to understand a man like Raoul Oman?

Quickly, before he could change his mind, Julia pressed the button for the fifteenth floor and waited as the car swooshed upward. Normally she *did* take the stairs, preferring to be more active. But the baby was more important than anything else, and she was following everything the doctor said to the letter. And it should still be all right, as long as she did her best to stay quiet and eat as much as her stomach could tolerate.

The tour of the fifteenth floor went reasonably well,

and they moved to the sixteenth without Raoul broaching more personal conversation.

As they passed the door of her own office, Julia's feet faltered when she saw the president of the company inside, staring at her desk with a kind of fierce concentration.

"Kane, is something wrong?" she asked.

"My meeting is finished," he said. "How was the tour, Raoul?"

"Ms. Parker has been most informative."

"Hmm. That's good. Fine."

Raoul lifted his eyebrows. He'd never seen Kane Haley so distracted. They'd met a number of years before, and both men had formed an immediate liking for the other. When the position of CFO had come available, Kane had immediately contacted him to see if he was interested.

He had been.

Raoul cast a glance at the slender blond-haired woman standing at his side. In no small way, Julia was responsible for his decision. She fascinated, annoyed and frustrated him beyond measure. While a part of him appreciated her reluctance for a more permanent arrangement, he couldn't help being intrigued.

Truly, he did not understand. Weren't all women anxious for those permanent bonds?

Certainly, the parade of marriageable women his mother had vexed him with had wanted everything that an alliance with the royal house would bring—wealth, power, position, the title of princess in a country whose princesses were revered and protected. The paparazzi would find no welcome in Hasan; the people would see to it.

Julia cleared her throat, apparently uncomfortable in

the silence. "Kane, I'm sure you have things you wanted to discuss with Mr. Oman. In the meantime I'll get back to work."

Kane gave her a peculiar look. "How have you been feeling, Julia?" he asked, ignoring her suggestion.

"Just fine," she assured, though she seemed confused by the inquiry.

"Somebody mentioned you'd been sick several times—in the restroom."

She jumped, and Raoul saw her hand hover over her stomach for an instant. "M-maybe once or twice. My system is a little sensitive after the Christmas holidays. You know, all that rich food. But I'm fine. I've even put on a few pounds."

This seemed to interest Kane almost as much as her supposed illness. "Yes, I guess you have."

Raoul frowned, wondering what nonsense his friend was pursuing. It was a matter for concern if a valued employee was suffering from ill-health, but anyone could see that Julia was fine. As for those "few pounds" she'd claimed, he'd noticed her figure was fuller and more enticing than ever, though it was well concealed by a heavy cashmere sweater.

Why western women were so concerned about weight was a mystery. Julia would be no less lovely if she gained a hundred pounds. Perhaps, though, the problem didn't lie with western women, but with western men who could not appreciate the beauty of a ripe, voluptuous body.

America was a confusing place. He'd spent many of his thirty-six years in the country, off and on, and still didn't always understand its ways.

He turned to Julia. "I will see you for dinner tonight.

I appreciate your offer to acquaint me with some of the Chicago food you have raved about.''

Julia's eyes narrowed. Things were going from bad to worse, but if Raoul thought he could manipulate her into having dinner with him, he was sadly mistaken. It would be awkward extricating herself in front of the company president, but she couldn't go out with Raoul. He was too compelling…too interested in the reason she'd left that Washington conference without a backward glance.

"That's a great idea," Kane Haley said before she could say anything. "But you'll both be my guests."

Huh?

Julia could tell that Raoul shared her confusion and they exchanged glances. She couldn't think of a single reason Kane would invite himself along, unless he was only thinking about visiting with an old friend.

"You know, I forgot I have an earlier commitment," she said. "But it doesn't matter, I'm sure you'll enjoy yourselves more without me."

"No." The two men uttered the protest in unison.

"You must dine with me tonight," Raoul insisted. "We have much news to share."

News?

No way was Julia going there.

The only "news" she had to share was something she didn't want him knowing in the first place. He was a proud man, and discovering she'd used him as a sperm donor wouldn't go over in a big way. It wouldn't matter that she'd felt desperate and had convinced herself he'd make her a beautiful baby; he'd be outraged.

With good reason, she acknowledged silently.

A familiar sense of guilt crowded Julia's throat, and she shifted uneasily.

"Really, I have other plans," she said. "Another time."

"Please cancel," Kane growled. Despite the "please" it sounded more like a command, and his face had the odd expression he'd gotten before, when he'd watched her talking to Maggie Steward. "I think we should properly welcome our new CFO to Chicago, don't you?"

"I—"

"I'd consider it a favor," he added.

A favor. Requested from the president. Sort of like a royal invitation you couldn't refuse.

"All right," Julia agreed reluctantly. "But there's something I'd better go check…with Mrs. Steward." She didn't have anything to check, but since they were all in her office, it was the only avenue of escape.

"Wait." Kane picked up something from her desk and handed it to her. "You're looking a little green, so you'd better take these. Raoul, we'll meet in your new office in say, fifteen minutes?" He stomped out, looking quite frustrated.

Julia's fingers closed around the package of crackers she'd been trying to swallow for lunch. What did crackers have to do with anything? And why would the president of the company be so concerned about the condition of her stomach?

"I take it you do not wish our relationship announced to the office," Raoul said after a moment.

She rolled her eyes, effectively distracted. "We don't have a relationship."

With a casual flick of his wrist, Raoul released the door so it swung closed. If it had been any other woman than Julia, he would have allowed the matter to drop. But the memory of her warm sensuality still invaded his sleep, though months had passed since he'd last held her.

He wasn't ready for marriage—he'd even left Hasan because of the pressure from his mother to start a family—but why shouldn't they enjoy one another? Particularly when their goal in remaining single seemed to be the same.

"I do not wish to make you uncomfortable, Julia, but nothing has changed...I still want you."

All at once the room seemed smaller and closer and Julia dragged needed air into her lungs. There was nothing menacing about the declaration, he was simply stating his desire.

The trouble was, she still wanted him, too.

Her body was practically screaming to touch him, and there wasn't a single thing she could do to make that need go away.

Chapter Two

"Please...don't," Julia said faintly.

"Shouldn't I be honest?"

It wasn't *Raoul's* honesty she was worried about. It was her own.

Darn it all, she'd told him he didn't need to worry about getting her pregnant, that it wasn't a problem! She'd said they could enjoy being together without bothering to use anything. The conference had continued for another three days and her ploy had worked. One month later she'd woken up, sick to her stomach and counting the days since her cycle should have started.

In other words, pregnant with a sheik's baby.

Her child would have all the advantages of Raoul's splendid genetics without her having to deal with the father. She'd just conveniently forgotten that the world really *was* a small place and that he could end up knowing about it after all.

"Perhaps Kane is correct, you do not look well,"

Raoul murmured, concerned at the pallor in her face. "Sit down, Julia."

"I don't need a mother hen," she said, sending him a scathing look. But she did as he'd requested, sinking into her chair with a sigh. "You're the last person I expected to see today."

"Kane made his selection for the position very quickly. It seemed best for the company."

Julia drummed her fingers on the surface of the desk. "How could you move to Chicago on such short notice? Don't you have family commitments?"

Raoul's lips tightened.

According to his family, his first concern should be to marry and produce children. His father was not so intolerable on the subject as his mother, but neither were pleased at his delay. They had fallen in love and married young themselves, and couldn't understand why he resisted their happy fate.

"My absence is not important. I have three brothers who help my father and grandfather in governing Hasan," he said.

"Oh." Julia seemed to be thinking his comment over with more concentration than it deserved. "What about sisters—do you have any?"

A smile eased the tension in Raoul's face. "Two. They are treasures to us all."

"But not in helping to govern the country, right? I suppose they have to wear robes and masks over their faces and not say anything except when spoken to?"

Perplexity creased the space between his eyes. He and Julia hadn't spoken of their personal lives when they'd met before, so in the ways that mattered most they did not know each other.

"There are many incorrect ideas about my country.

Women in Hasan do not wear the chador," he explained. "They are as free as their western counterparts. Perhaps more free, because our men do not have the same limited views of feminine beauty."

Julia didn't look convinced. "Your sisters—"

"Have no interest in ruling Hasan," he said, having had this discussion with more than one American woman. "Jasmine is an artist who wishes to be left alone to work—she will not even act as our cultural minister. And Fatima is a doctor. She occupies a position similar to your surgeon general, but spends most of her time treating patients."

"I see."

Raoul glanced at his watch. He would prefer staying to talk with Julia, but he was expected in that meeting. "I'll see you later," he said. "Perhaps Kane will change his mind about going to dinner with us and we can be alone."

Color flooded back into Julia's face with extraordinary speed and her eyes flashed in annoyance. "Oh, *yes*," she mocked. "My 'invitation' to help you sample Chicago's cuisine."

"You raved about your pizza and Italian beef sandwiches when we met in Washington. You said—"

"I don't care what I said," she snapped.

He chuckled. She had such fire, he adored that part of her. "You would not have agreed if I had simply asked."

"So true."

"So I ensured you couldn't refuse."

Her eyes grew frosty, even remote, and Raoul looked at her in puzzlement. "I've already had enough men thinking they know what's best for everyone else,"

Julia said evenly, but she was plainly furious. "I won't let anybody control me."

Obviously he wasn't accomplishing anything by staying, so Raoul gave her a courteous bow and opened the door again. "It may have seemed that I was trying to do that, but I wasn't. We will speak later, when you are feeling…better."

Something hit the door as he closed it behind him, and he wondered what Julia had thrown. Nothing too dangerous, he decided with a small smile.

He liked this Julia even better than the temptress he had known in Washington. She was just as seductive, but there were depths he'd only glimpsed during their tempestuous few days together.

Depths he wanted to explore.

We will speak later, when you are feeling…better.
Better.

Julia practically snorted. He'd meant *logical.* Or *sensible.* Or some other male notion about the return of reason to an irrational woman. She willed herself to calm down, certain so much emotion couldn't be good for either her or the baby. And the worst part was knowing she'd brought the whole thing on herself.

Sitting back in her chair, she put a hand over her abdomen and practiced her deep breathing.

Her life had changed so much since she'd had that June appointment with the gynecologist. She'd felt herself going cold while hearing the results of the tests, but the doctor just kept talking. Just kept explaining. Saying that endometriosis usually got worse, that a pregnancy might relieve the symptoms, or even eliminate them. But, as time passed her chance of conceiving a baby would grow less and less…that it was probably a condition she'd had since first starting her periods.

Julia shuddered, thinking about her childhood.

She'd been so frightened of her father, a loud, over-bearing army officer who controlled his household with the same iron fist he used to control the men under his command. She'd tried to tell him how much her menstrual periods hurt, but he'd told her to stop whining. Pain was an illusion.

"Some illusion," she muttered.

The worst part was that she'd finally accepted his iron-man philosophy, deciding she just had a low threshold for pelvic pain and shouldn't complain. Maybe it wouldn't have changed anything to know the truth earlier, but she would have been prepared.

The phone rang, making her jump, and she reached for the receiver, happy to think about anything but the mess she'd made for herself.

"Yes?"

"How did it go?" Maggie Steward's soft, concerned tones were a balm to Julia.

"Lousy," she admitted. "God, I've done something really stupid. And insensitive and insane."

"This afternoon?"

"No. Over six months ago."

"So Sheik Oman is the…" Her friend's voice trailed and she sighed. "Okay. Let's have dinner tonight and we'll talk about it."

"I can't." Julia stabbed a pen at her daily planner. "Raoul announced that *I'd* invited him to dinner, right in front of Kane. Before I could tell him to take a hike, Kane jumped in and said he'd take us both."

"Really?"

"Really. What's wrong with that boss of yours

lately? He's been really strange. You should have heard his inquisition about me being sick in the restroom.''

"He's your boss, too.'' Maggie's tone was prim, the way she sometimes got when she was protecting Kane. She never let her hair down, so to speak, when it came to the president of the company.

"He's not my boss, he's my boss's boss,'' Julia said fliply.

"Is that supposed to make a difference?''

"I guess not.''

Despite the stress of the past two hours, a smile crept across Julia's face. Maggie was only a few years older than herself, but she certainly knew how to put an impertinent employee in her place. At least she knew how to put an employee named Julia Parker in her place.

"Look, Maggie, I have to work this out on my own. But thanks for the support.''

"Are you going to be all right?''

"You bet.'' Julia dropped the receiver back in its cradle, shaking her head at the outrageous falsehood.

Her image of a sheik from the Middle East had been abysmally vague. She never would have guessed that Raoul Oman was the king's son, rather than being a distant cousin or something. Now she knew and it complicated an already complicated situation.

Soon she'd have to make up her mind how to tell Raoul that she was pregnant…and that the baby was his.

She could imagine how well that piece of news would go over.

"Is this all right, Julia?''

"Fine,'' she muttered, sitting down at the restaurant table. Both Kane and Raoul had been painfully attentive since they'd left the office and she was sick to death of it.

Are you warm enough?

I'm fine. She'd shown Raoul her coat but he'd just frowned.

It's January and there is snow on the ground. You should wear something heavier.

As she got out of his Jaguar, Kane had rushed around, a fierce expression on his face as he grabbed her arm. *Be careful. Don't slip on the ice, you could hurt yourself.*

Between Raoul's hot glances and the peculiar way Kane was acting, Julia was ready to scream, and they hadn't even given the waiter their order. She only hoped she could get through the evening without tossing her cookies. When Raoul had suggested they go to an Italian restaurant for some of Chicago's famous pizza she'd smiled and gulped.

Pizza wasn't the ideal food for a pregnant woman still coping with all-day morning sickness.

Together Raoul and Kane argued about the merits of the Chicago Bulls and the Dallas Cowboys, an argument she'd ignore at the best of times. After a few minutes they consulted her about the pizza and she shrugged. "Anything you like," she answered. It really didn't matter, since nothing connected to a pizza would sit well on her stomach.

"Would you like some wine?" It was Raoul's question, but for some reason Kane looked particularly interested in her answer.

"No alcohol, right, Julia?" he prompted after a moment. "It wouldn't be good for you."

"I...no, just milk," she said, knowing she needed

to get something in her stomach for the sake of the baby.

Kane gave her another odd stare, and she lifted an eyebrow. She'd never had a great deal of contact with Kane Haley, but now he was acting like her den mother or something.

She sighed, more exhausted than at any other time in her life. Being pregnant was harder work than she'd ever thought it would be, but at night, when she was thinking about the coming baby, she knew it was worth everything.

"Have you found a place to live?" she asked Raoul. The waiter had brought milk for her and coffee for the men. It was warm in the restaurant and she'd nearly fallen asleep—quite a feat, considering the tensions swirling around the table.

"I've temporarily settled at a hotel."

Raoul swallowed some of his coffee with an effort. It would have been rude to tell the restaurant that their coffee had the strength of dishwater. His tastes were somewhat different from American preferences.

"You should buy a house out in the Northshore area," Kane said. "Nice houses out there. If nothing else, it's a good investment."

"I have no wish for a family home."

His friend shrugged. "Sometimes families are thrust upon us, whether we like it or not."

A soft gasp came from Julia and her hand jerked. She tried to catch her milk from toppling on the table, with only marginal success. Liquid splattered liberally and Kane jumped up to get more napkins from their waiter.

She sputtered an apology, her face nearly as white as the milk. Raoul placed his hand over her damp fingers in an attempt to calm her. "It is all right, *chère,*" he said quietly. "There is no harm."

"No." She shook her head. "That is, I'm just over-reacting."

"Overreacting to what?"

"To…" Her voice trailed and she shrugged. "Nothing. Kane is right, I haven't been feeling well. I should go home."

"I'll call for a taxi."

"No." Julia's protest fell on blank air, because Raoul had already disappeared. For an instant, the need to assert her independence warred with the desire to escape. Tarnation, she could call her own cab. She was perfectly capable of managing on her own, and she didn't need someone playing the big strong rescuer.

There wasn't any time to think about it though, because Kane returned with the waiter, who began cleaning up the mess she'd made.

"Where's Raoul?" Kane asked.

"Calling a cab," Raoul answered as he approached the table. "It is outside, waiting. Julia isn't well and I am escorting her home."

"Oh." Kane frowned as he glanced at her. "Stomach again?"

"Something like that."

"Do you need help?"

The inquiry was directed at his friend, not Julia, and her temper flared. "I don't need help from either one of you," she growled. "Believe it or not, I've survived quite well on my own since I was seventeen."

"I could not let you go alone," Raoul said, sounding appalled. "It isn't done."

Julia sucked in a breath. *Men.* "Maybe not in Hasan, but here in America—"

"I agree with Raoul," Kane interrupted. "One of us will see you home."

"That would be my privilege," Raoul insisted.

Kane looked ready to argue, then shrugged. "All right, I'll see you tomorrow."

It wasn't all right with Julia, but once again Raoul had placed her in a difficult position. If she insisted on leaving by herself she'd look like a shrew in front of Kane Haley, so she managed to grit her teeth and not say anything at all.

In the lobby, Raoul looked out at the lightly falling snow and pulled a scarf from his pocket. He turned to Julia, prepared for a battle.

"You must put this around your neck—you're not dressed for such weather."

Her stubborn chin lifted. "I'm sure the cab is heated."

"You should not get chilled, particularly when you aren't feeling well."

"Raoul…don't push."

The tired plea cut straight to his heart, but he shook his head and drew the silk scarf around her neck. It wasn't thick enough in such weather, but it would help protect her throat. He would have put his own coat around her, but knew he would lose such an effort. Julia was as skittish as one of his colts back home and she could only be pushed so far. At least she had gloves to wear, though he couldn't see how the stylishly thin leather could provide the necessary warmth.

Kane was dealing with the bill, so Raoul nodded a farewell to his friend and took Julia's arm.

"It may be slippery," he murmured when she tried to shake free.

"I'm more accustomed to walking on ice than you are—or do you have an annual snowfall in Hasan?"

He chuckled. "No snow."

She plainly wasn't happy, but he held her firmly as they walked to the taxicab. Hasanian women were fiercely independent in their own way, but they willingly accepted the courtesies required by male honor.

"Really, you don't have to come with me," Julia insisted as she slid onto the vehicle seat, and he followed.

"I don't have all night," said the cab driver. "I go off shift in half an hour. What's your address, lady?"

Raoul's eyes narrowed and he looked every bit an imperious sheik, ruler of his world. "You will wait as long as necessary, is that clear?"

"Yes, sir." The man ran a finger under his collar and scrunched down farther in the front seat.

Julia sighed. There wasn't any point in fighting the issue. One way or the other Raoul was coming with her and she might as well get it over with. She gave the driver her address, certain that Raoul would remember both the number and street name. Whatever else he was, he wasn't stupid, and he was determined to get his answers about their brief affair.

When the taxi pulled into the driveway of her nineteenth-century brick house, set well back from the street, she squared her shoulders. "Uh…thanks. I'll see you at work."

A soft laugh came from Raoul as he took the fare from his wallet. "I will see you inside, and call another cab after you're settled."

"No."

"Yes, Julia." His tone, though gentle, didn't brook

disagreement, and she simply didn't have the energy to start another argument.

"Fine," she muttered.

Lord, she was tired. Too tired to fight, which was frightening. It was too easy to let someone else take control, to find yourself struggling for an identity. Raoul was exactly the sort of man she'd vowed to keep out of her life, and here he was, square in the middle of it.

The interior of her house was chilly, and she hurried to the thermostat and pushed it higher.

"Go lie down," Raoul murmured. "I will fix you something warm to drink."

Julia found herself obeying before she could even think. In the bedroom she threw off her skirt and sweater and deliberately pulled on a thick velour nightgown that covered her from her neck to her toes—a far cry from the scraps of lace and silk she'd worn during their time in Washington.

Still...she looked at herself in the mirror and decided that even without the less-than-romantic nightwear, she was hardly a candidate for seduction. Her skin was pale, her medium-length shag-cut hair was stringy around her face, and there were dark circles beneath her eyes. The extra tiredness was natural. After all, she was pregnant and she'd never expected to see Raoul again. He'd stormed back into her world with the subtleness of a lovesick camel.

Muppet, her five-year-old black-and-white cat, was curled up on the bedroom fireplace hearth. He got up and stretched when she crawled under the down comforter, then wiggled his way under the sheet to settle next to her stomach.

"Hello," she whispered, running her fingers through

his fur. He purred, and the comforting rumble eased some of the tension in her body.

When Raoul left she would have to force herself to eat and drink more milk. It was like a mantra these days. *Eat. Eat. Eat.* Drink gallons of milk. And pray the baby gained weight. She'd taken her prenatal vitamins that morning, so....

Julia's eyes flew open.

The vitamins.

She tried to remember where she'd left them. If they were on the kitchen counter, then the secret was probably out. Alarmed, she slid from the bed and went into the bathroom, gratefully closing her fingers around the bottle sitting on the vanity.

"Julia?"

"I'll be right out." Quickly she thrust the bottle into a drawer.

Raoul had placed a tray on her bedside table, and he watched as she hurried across the room. Despite the condition of her stomach and nerves, Julia felt a curl of heat in her abdomen. She'd never expected to be in a bedroom with Raoul Oman again, and it was harder to ignore the memories in such a private setting.

And, while she couldn't tell what Raoul was thinking, there was a certain intensity in his posture that suggested he was remembering, too.

"I prepared tinned soup and tea," he said. "Get under your blankets before you become chilled."

"I turned the heat up."

Raoul kept the smile from his face, knowing it would simply annoy Julia. There had been many surprises about her that day, and her house was another. It was a beautifully restored brick bungalow from the 1800s, with a simple, restful decor that belied the cool sophistication she projected.

"I hope you don't object, but I made myself a cup of coffee," he said when she was settled in her bed, resting against a pile of pillows. "But I thought you would prefer the tea I found by your stove. Herbal, I think."

Julia's eyelids fluttered open, and she looked at him, so pale and beautiful that he wanted to pull her into his arms. Their time together had been so brief, yet it seemed that every cell in his body was imprinted with her warmth and scent. Sometimes at night he woke, thinking she was there, and the desire was so strong he would be unable to sleep again.

"You're welcome to the coffee," she whispered. "I don't mean to be...ungracious."

"I didn't say you were."

He wanted to pursue the reason she'd eluded him following the Washington conference, but he couldn't. Not when she was so vulnerable. Something told him Julia would only resent him for taking advantage, making things more difficult later.

The blankets next to her stirred as she reached for the cup of soup and a furry head poked itself out. Julia stroked the feline's head with an absent caress and it settled down, watching Raoul with unblinking eyes.

"Your cat seems suspicious."

"Muppet is protective."

"Ah, the jealous type...I can understand. He is in an enviable position—one I wouldn't relinquish easily."

Raoul could see the muscles in Julia's throat convulse. He'd given her a reminder of his interest, a reminder she understood. Truly, he couldn't comprehend why she'd acted one way at the conference—a bold temptress with flashing gold eyes and a sassy smile— and now was so reticent. It was a woman's prerogative to invite or cast a man from her bed, but this did not make sense.

Still musing on the mystery, Raoul sat on the end of the mattress while he drank his coffee. It wasn't the Arabic blend he liked best, but at least he'd brewed it at the proper strength.

Julia took small sips of her soup, keeping her gaze cast downward. She was so strong, he disliked seeing her so quiet and withdrawn. Despite her denials, could she really be sick? Something serious?

A chill that had nothing to do with a Chicago winter went through him. Julia had looked well earlier, her color bright with anger, but that didn't mean there was nothing amiss with her health. When Raoul couldn't stand wondering any longer, he leaned forward.

"Is Kane correct—are you ill?" he asked. "More than your excuse about recovering from rich holiday food?"

The tip of her tongue flicked over her lips and she put her teacup back on the tray. "I'm fine. Anyway, you don't have to worry, I'm not your concern."

"We were lovers," he reminded. "Do you think I care so little for the women I take to my bed?"

"I…" Julia drew a shaky breath.

We were lovers.

The words reverberated in her heart and mind. They had engaged in the most intimate of acts between a man and woman. She hadn't wanted to feel pleasure, wanting to think of it as a medical procedure and nothing more, but she'd burned when Raoul Oman touched her. A burning she'd never come close to feeling with another man.

"Never mind, *chère*," Raoul murmured. He put his cup on the tray next to her empty soup bowl, then moved both to the top of her dresser.

Tell him.

Her conscience was darned inconvenient, but Julia opened her mouth to the unspoken command. "Raoul, we…I…"

We're having a baby and I planned it all along.

"Rest now. I'll arrange for you to see a doctor tomorrow."

Irritation swamped less-comfortable emotions, and she pushed herself farther upright against the headboard. "You'll do no such thing. I don't need to see a doctor, and I don't need you to take care of me."

For some reason Raoul's dark eyes gleamed with satisfaction. "Perhaps."

"Perhaps nothing. I told you, I've been—"

"Yes," he interrupted smoothly. "You've been taking care of yourself since you were seventeen."

"That's right." Keeping a wary eye on him, Julia snatched the telephone and dialed the taxi company. She asked that a cab be sent to her house as quickly as possible. "They'll be here in twenty minutes," she said, returning the receiver to the cradle. It was remarkably fast service considering the weather, but twenty minutes still seemed like twenty years.

Raoul sat next to her on the bed, his leg nudging her hip, as though he had all the time in the world. "You don't have a family, Julia?"

"Just a father and a brother," she muttered. "My mother died when I was four. I barely remember her."

"Your father and brother, you are not close to them?"

"Not in this lifetime." Her mouth twisted in a grimace. "My brother is a gung ho Navy Seal—sudden death in every direction. He's older than me, and we never had much in common. We only see each other every couple of years."

"And your father?"

"I haven't seen him since I was seventeen. I'm a disappointment, you see. A weak female who wouldn't toughen up and do what he wanted. He washed his hands of me when I left for college instead of enlisting in his army."

Raoul fought a surge of anger at the bleak expression on Julia's face. His own family's gentle tyranny about marriage and children seemed minor by comparison. How could her father fail to recognize the unique strength of the daughter he'd raised?

"He is a fool," Raoul said flatly.

Faint surprise registered in her eyes. "He'd argue the point with you—he's very well thought of by the Pentagon. Last I heard, he'd become a three-star general."

"That is merely a title. It doesn't make him less of a fool. A blind man could see that you are not weak. You have the heart of a tigress."

Julia blinked several times. She would have expected a man like Raoul to defend her father, at least in part, but instead he was supporting her without reservation. A traitorous warmth crept through her body.

"Thank you," she murmured. A yawn caught her by surprise and she sighed. "Sorry."

Raoul regarded her for a long minute. "You are tired, *chère*. I will wait for the taxi in the other room."

He leaned closer. His finger stroked the arch of one eyebrow, then traced the curve of her cheek, and a flood of remembered sensations made her tremble. She couldn't have spoken if her life depended upon the words.

"I thought you couldn't possibly be as lovely as I remembered, but I was wrong."

The dark, gravelly quality of his voice hypnotized Julia to the point that she didn't object when he brushed her mouth with his. The light kiss deepened and she sensed the suppressed sexual energy in him, yet even that wasn't enough to make her pull away. Their brief time together had made her far too susceptible to his potent brand of loving.

"Sleep well," he murmured. "Please think about seeing a doctor if you're not better soon."

"I...yes." Julia tried to be glad Raoul was too much of a gentleman to attempt a seduction when he believed she was ill. She might manage to actually *feel* glad in an hour or so.

A moment later he'd closed the door behind him and she curled onto her side, a tear trickling down her cheek. These days she was a confused muddle of pregnancy hormones. Everything was blown out of proportion, her emotions seesawing wildly.

But things would be better in the morning.

They had to be.

Chapter Three

"No more foolishness," Julia mumbled around the toothbrush in her mouth. She spat a foamy mouthful into the sink and rinsed.

She'd escaped her usual bout of morning sickness, even managing to eat a bowl of cereal and drink a glass of milk. After the previous day that was a miracle, since tense emotions usually made the nausea worse.

And *nothing* about Raoul Oman was calm and soothing.

She'd had a moment of weakness the previous night, but that moment was over. The baby was the most important thing in her life, and she wouldn't do anything to jeopardize it.

Julia put a hand over her abdomen. Over the past few months she'd worn looser clothing at work, choosing soft, thick sweaters to conceal the rounding of her stomach, rather than her usual silk blouses and suits. Sooner or later it wouldn't be enough to conceal her secret any longer, and the news would be out. She only prayed it would be good news.

Sometime during the night Julia had realized she would have to tell Raoul, preferably before gossip spread through the company with its usual wildfire speed. He was extremely intelligent. He'd know the baby was his, so the best way of handling the matter was to tell him first and hope for the best. She'd make it clear she didn't want anything from him, so maybe he wouldn't care.

"Yeah, right," she muttered.

The funny thing was, she didn't have any idea how Raoul would react. Naturally there would be shock in the beginning, but after that?

She shivered, though the house was quite warm. The doorbell interrupted her troubling thoughts, and she stepped into the living room. Peering through a window, she gulped at the sight of Raoul standing on her doorstep.

"Oh, Lord," she breathed.

It was the perfect opportunity to talk with him privately, but having that particular conversation in her home probably wasn't smart. Later would be best, at the office, or maybe in a restaurant. In a public location, after she'd had time to think about her announcement—and his possible reactions—for a little longer.

"What are you doing here?" she asked as she opened the door.

Raoul smiled, pleased to see the color in Julia's cheeks. She was lovely, her dark-blond hair falling around her face in the stylish cut she favored. "Good morning, *chère*."

"I asked you to stop calling me that."

"So you did. There are many beautiful Arabic words

of affection. Would it please you more if I chose an endearment from my native language?''

"Not especially," she growled.

Chuckling, he motioned with the key he had taken from her key ring before leaving the previous evening. "I brought your car back from the office. I did not want you inconvenienced because we took a cab home from the restaurant.''

"Oh. You didn't have to do that.''

She seemed so surprised that Raoul's mouth tightened. What kind of men had Julia known that she would be surprised by something so small? He'd gotten a clear idea of her father and brother, an idea that wasn't flattering. Were there others who had acted just as badly?

"How are you feeling this morning?'' he asked, deciding not to upset her with questions she'd already demonstrated she didn't want to answer.

"Fine." Her chin lifted. "If you'll wait while I get my coat and purse, we can go in together.''

"Shouldn't you be resting?''

"No, I'm all right.'' Julia disappeared, then returned, pulling on her coat. She locked the door and turned around. "Ready?''

The falsely cheerful tone of her voice didn't fool Raoul. Though she was plainly in better health today, there was a distinct tension in her body and face.

The snow that had fallen during the night made the footing treacherous, and Raoul put a hand on Julia's elbow. Fortunately, the winding, snow-lined streets of the neighborhood had already been tended by city employees, making them safe to drive now that the storm had blown over.

When they reached the car he held up the key once more. "Do you wish to drive, or shall I?"

Again, surprise registered in her hazel-gold eyes. "Er...no, go ahead."

There were so many mysteries about Julia. Raoul shook his head as he closed the passenger door and crossed to the driver's side of the vehicle. In Washington they had shared a great passion—an uncomplicated passion in many ways. Though he'd sensed deeper currents within his mischievously sensual lover, they'd been well protected.

"Tell me something about the people at Kane Haley, Inc.," he asked, deciding it was a safe topic, and might help Julia relax. "I've met a few, and reviewed the employee records, but that's all."

"Well, Margaret Steward is Kane's administrative assistant. She's extremely competent and knows the company from top to bottom. She's great to go to when you have questions or problems. Matthew Holder and Jennifer Martin just got married and they have a baby, but she's out on maternity leave. Sharon Davies recently married Jack Waterton, who's one of our big clients. Sharon and I've been...." At the swift intake of Julia's breath, Raoul glanced at her and saw she was more tense than ever.

"Yes?"

"N-nothing. You know Kane, of course."

"We met when I was attending the Sorbonne."

"You didn't go to Oxford?" Julia turned in her seat, nervously adjusting the seat belt over her waist. "I thought it was the school of choice for wealthy Middle-Eastern families."

"I did attend university in England. But as a compromise to *Grand-mère,* my post-graduate studies were completed in France at the Sorbonne.''

"That's nice. I worked my way through school at a tiny college here in the midwest. Nobody's ever heard of it."

Raoul lifted one of his eyebrows. Julia's tone challenged him, as if she expected him to disapprove of her education. "It must have been difficult working and going to classes. You're highly thought of at the company. I assume this tiny college contributed to your exceptional skills, though I believe you would excel regardless.''

"Thank you."

Julia sighed, still rattled by her earlier slip. She'd nearly said something about her pregnancy when she was telling him about Sharon and Jennifer. She wasn't sure about anything any longer. Deceiving Raoul had been wrong, but she'd rejected the possibility of a sperm bank, and none of the men she knew were candidates for fatherhood.

They arrived at the office, and Raoul regarded her with a grave expression as they stepped into the elevator. "Julia, are you certain you're well enough to work?''

She tried to summon anger at his comment, but since genuine concern seemed to be motivating Raoul, it wasn't easy.

"I'm sure. Why?"

He held out her key, smiling faintly. "You wanted me to drive your car. I thought American women did not appreciate a man taking control, even in such a small matter.''

Her mouth dropped open and, just as quickly, Julia snapped it closed. "I thought men, especially from your part of world, would assume a woman couldn't possibly be a competent driver.''

"That is not one of my faults.'' Raoul's gaze lingered on her lips, and just like that, she got breathless. "It appears we have much to learn of each other, don't we, *bien-aimée?*''

The morning flew, though Julia was distracted by the memory of Raoul's words and the warmth in his eyes.

Okay, so he played the game well.

Lots of men pretended they were the new and improved version of the old nineties man. It didn't mean they were. She was even willing to concede that some members of the male sex actually *were* sensitive and liberated. But she'd always seemed to attract a certain kind of man—the kind that wanted a Victorian-era woman they could control.

"Earth to Julia,'' teased a voice and Julia looked up to see Sharon Waterton at the door of her office.

"Hello, *Mrs.* Waterton,'' Julia returned with a smile. Sharon had become much more open since her marriage. And, since she was pregnant as well, they were sharing some of the joys and woes of the condition—though in Sharon's case, it wasn't a secret any longer.

"Jennifer came in with the baby. They're in the lunchroom, and I'm going down to see her,'' Sharon announced. "Why don't you come with me?''

Julia looked at the stack of work on her desk and thought about the dozen phone calls that she needed to make by the end of the day. On the other hand, she loved holding little Jason. He was so sweet; it made her think of the moment when she'd hold her own child.

"Sure, I could use a break.''

Tossing a pencil on the desk, Julia stood and adjusted her heavy, oversized sweater. Thanks to Raoul's arrival, she was more conscious than ever of her swelling stomach.

"You don't show that much," Sharon assured. "You have one of those bodies that conceals it longer. Not like me. I'm all out in front. Jack is so excited about the baby he keeps buying me maternity dresses. I have more than I'll ever be able to wear. Not to mention all the things he's gotten for the baby."

For a moment Julia envied the other woman. There was something so...*settled* about Sharon's life. She was obviously crazy about her husband, and Jack Waterton couldn't hide his devotion to his wife. They seemed like a perfect couple.

"Let Jack buy anything he wants," Julia said quietly. "It makes him happy. Anyway, not showing is a mixed blessing."

Sharon sighed. "I'm sure it'll be all right. And it isn't as if you don't show. You know, it's really tricky guessing if someone is pregnant, or if they've just put on some weight. Remember that woman down in the coffee shop? She's looked pregnant for the last three years."

Julia smiled obligingly. Trying not to let her turbulent emotions show, she followed Sharon to the elevator. In the break room Jennifer and the baby were surrounded by a small group of admiring employees, so it was several minutes before Julia had a chance to hold Jason.

He blew a bubble at her and she blinked back tears. Babies were so precious. They stole your heart with ridiculous ease. No matter how Raoul reacted about her own child, she couldn't be sorry about her pregnancy.

It would have been heartbreaking to have been surrounded by her friends as they became mothers, and to wonder if she'd ever be a mother herself.

A murmur of male voices prompted Julia to look up...and her gaze collided with Raoul's. Next to him stood Kane Haley, who seemed equally riveted by the sight of her holding a blanket-swathed infant in her arms.

"Since when did you get so interested in children?" Kane murmured.

Warmth crept up Julia's neck. Honestly, Kane was getting stranger and stranger. "I've always loved kids," she replied. She returned Jason to his mother, and stepped away from the crowd. "You know I'm on the day-care committee."

"Mmm...that's right," he said.

Raoul frowned. "Perhaps Julia could show the facility to me. Somehow, we missed seeing this child-care center during our tour."

Something in his dark gaze made Julia squirm all over again. "I didn't think you'd be interested," she muttered. "You aren't a family man. And besides, it isn't finished yet."

"Then you can tell me about it."

Kane murmured something and left, a strained look on his face. Raoul barely gave his departing friend a glance. He had new questions about Julia, but he thought he might be closer to the answers. The tenderness in her face when she'd held the baby had told him a great deal, as well as her comment that he wasn't a family man.

He guided her into an empty room, then blocked the exit and crossed his arms over his chest.

"You ended our affair because I made it clear I

didn't desire children, at least not for some time," he announced, certain this was the explanation.

Julia's eyes widened, and he saw a flash of panic in their golden depths, followed by rueful humor. "Uh…no."

"Do not deny you want a family. It is obvious how much you care about children."

"Don't be ridiculous. Of course I love kids," she snapped.

"Yes, and I told you I wasn't planning to marry for a number of years. So—"

"So, nothing." She made a disgusted sound. "Trust me, I *don't* want to ever get married. Your lack of interest had nothing to do with breaking things off between us."

Raoul tried not to be insulted. He'd grown accustomed to being the subject of determined matrimonial pursuit, so it was disconcerting to hear Julia so adamant, even though her sentiments about remaining single mirrored his own. Besides, she hadn't said she didn't want to marry *him*, she just didn't want to marry, period.

He'd jumped to a conclusion that was obviously wrong, but his frustration was building. They'd desired each other with equal passion, so she wasn't bored with him as a lover. He could have seduced her the previous evening when she'd responded to him, but mere seduction wasn't enough.

"Perhaps we should continue our discussion upstairs?"

Julia was starting to look cornered, but he made a gesture with his hand that didn't brook disagreement.

"You're really annoying," she muttered as she slid past him.

"Is that so?"

"It always has to be your way, doesn't it?" Julia faced him in the hallway and there was a shade of bitterness in her voice that he'd never heard before.

"Wanting an explanation is reasonable. It has nothing to do with having things my way."

"I explained."

"But not with the complete truth."

She swallowed. He could see the muscles working in her throat, and for an instant his determination wavered. He didn't want to hurt Julia; he cared about her.

"You're just upset because you weren't the one calling the shots," she said. "It's probably the first time a woman ever ended an affair with you, instead of the other way around."

Raoul sighed. In a way, Julia was right. He'd always been careful when choosing his lovers, and his relationships usually ended by mutual consent. But not always. There had been a few times of tears and demands from a woman who had come to hope for more than he wished to give. Now he was faced with a woman who had not only said goodbye first, she'd done everything possible to ensure he wouldn't contact her again.

"There is something to what you're saying," he admitted. "But I still want an answer."

And I still want you in my bed.

Somehow, he didn't think he should say that part aloud. He'd already told Julia he wanted her. The decision was hers. No matter what else happened, he would never do anything to force or frighten her.

"Let's have lunch together," she said finally. "There *is* something we should...discuss."

"All right. I'm ready to leave right now."

Another flash of resentment darkened her eyes, and he sighed; he'd never realized she had so much prickly independence. "I will meet you in your office in an hour—is that acceptable, *chère?*"

"Does it matter?" Without waiting for an answer, Julia turned on her heel and hurried down the corridor.

Raoul frowned thoughtfully as he returned to the fifteenth floor. His corner office looked out on the River West part of Chicago, and was nicely furnished. He'd had framed photos from Hasan hung on the walls, and he stood for a while, gazing at them. His favorite was of sunrise on the desert, suffused with gold and pink and mysterious shadows. The desert was unpredictable, ever-changing, filled with beauty…just like Julia.

Though it disturbed him to have his thoughts dominated by this stubborn creature, he couldn't deny the way she made him feel. Julia was the most compelling, tempting woman he'd ever known. It could take a lifetime to understand her.

A lifetime?

A grim smile tugged at Raoul's mouth. For a determined bachelor, he was certainly playing with fire.

Julia completed most of her phone calls before the appointed hour for lunch with Raoul. It was crazy, but each time he pushed, she pushed right back. Hard. Considering the secret she was planning to reveal to him, it wasn't the smartest thing she'd ever done.

Of course, she wouldn't tell him everything. She'd simply say she'd gotten pregnant, despite using birth control. She hated lying, but it seemed best…if he believed her.

When the knock came on her door she expected to

see Raoul, instead it was Kane Haley. She motioned him inside.

"Is there something you wanted, Kane?"

He seemed distinctly uncomfortable. "I understand you've advised several clients, including the McKay Group, to put in child-care facilities."

She frowned. "It's part of my job to give sound management advice. And providing on-site child care *is* the right step to take if you want to recruit and keep the best employees. I assume that's why you're investing in a center here at the company?"

"Yes."

Julia glanced at her watch, then looked up to see Raoul appear in the doorway behind Kane. Great. Regular as clockwork. For someone who prided herself on carefully managing her life, she was in big trouble. His eyes laughed at her silently, so at least he was in a better mood than he'd been earlier.

"Is there anything else, Kane?" she murmured. "I—"

"No...*yes*," he said abruptly. He looked ready to explode, more frustrated than she'd ever seen him. "I know you're pregnant, Julia. Who is the father?"

I know you're pregnant...

Raoul stared at Julia. Her cheeks had turned white, every trace of color erased. She'd begun to stand, but now slid into her chair as if she didn't have the strength to remain upright.

"W-what?" she whispered.

"You're pregnant. It all adds up. The nausea, the weight gain, the crackers," Kane ticked each detail off on his fingers. "Everyone knows pregnant women eat crackers when they have morning sickness."

"What are you talking about?" Raoul demanded.

Startled, Kane whipped around. "Raoul, I didn't know you were there."

"Obviously. You are basing your assumptions on crackers?" Raoul asked, though he had a sickening sensation that his friend knew exactly what he was talking about.

Though Kane was plainly embarrassed, he shook his head. "Not just that. Julia wouldn't drink wine at the restaurant, she wanted milk. *Milk.* And she's been passionate about the day-care center, advising all her clients to install one."

"Not all of them," Julia breathed.

"Enough. You cup your abdomen a lot, did you realize that Julia? Almost protectively. I've noticed pregnant women do that—maybe it's an instinct, or something."

Raoul remembered seeing Julia do exactly that, placing her palm over her lower stomach in a protective gesture. He hadn't thought anything about it, not after hearing she'd been ill recently. But it also made sense if she were having a baby.

"Who's the father?" Kane asked with quiet insistence. "How far along are you?"

She flicked her tongue over her lips, visibly shaken. "Almost seven months. And it's not...if you're worried something inappropriate happened, it's nothing like that."

Kane rolled his eyes in disbelief. "Pregnant women are bigger at seven months."

"*Almost* seven months, and the baby is underweight," she said, her voice wobbly. "Quite underweight. But it should be all right. The doctor is monitoring us closely and I'm doing everything he tells me."

"Are you sure it's seven months? Is it possible you went…someplace? In early fall? That is, one of those, um, places?"

Raoul didn't have the faintest notion what Kane was trying to ask in such an uncharacteristically awkward manner, but after a long look at Julia's guilt-filled face, he turned to Kane.

"If Julia is seven months pregnant, then she is carrying my child," he said harshly. The enormity of what he was saying reverberated through his head, and he gritted his teeth. Damn it, he didn't want to be a father. Not for a long while. He'd even left Hasan to stop his mother's incessant fussing to do exactly what Julia had apparently already accomplished.

"Yours?" Kane's gaze narrowed. "You're certain?"

"We met at a Washington, D.C., business conference in June. We were…intimate. We haven't spoken about it, but I have no doubt the child is mine. Isn't that right, Julia?"

She hesitated, then shrugged, a defeated look in her eyes. "Raoul is the father."

Still looking doubtful, Kane turned to Julia. "You're sure about the seven months?"

"For pity's sake, talk to the head of the department," she cried. "I told Carol I'd need maternity leave sometime in March, but not to say anything until I was ready to make an announcement."

His gaze narrowed for a long moment, then he shook his head as if making up his mind about something. "I'll do that."

Kane left hastily, and it was a long minute before Raoul could look at Julia, much less speak. "Shall we go? I am certain you should eat, since you are now eating for *two*."

Julia drew a small breath, trying to take in enough air to clear her mind. It didn't take a genius to know Raoul was upset—the rigidity in his handsome features and the set of his shoulders told her exactly how much.

"Raoul—"

"We will continue this away from the office, Julia," he said harshly. "I do not wish to discuss it here."

"I'm not going anywhere with you looking like that," she said. His face was unsmiling and remote, and Julia's heart ached for some unaccountable reason. As unsettling as his sensual teasing had been, this was much worse.

"What is wrong with how I look?"

She sighed. "Just close the door. You can say whatever you want to say without anyone hearing. I think we've had enough unintended bombshells today."

"Fine." The door closed with a snap. "I assume you planned to tell me that I am going to be a father?"

Julia took a moment before answering. "Yes...but I don't want anything from you, I just thought you should know."

"You said you were using something—that there wasn't any danger. For that matter, you said it was the wrong time of the month. I realize now that you didn't *want* me to use protection, did you?"

"I'm sorry, I just...wanted a baby," she whispered.

"In other words, you used me to get pregnant."

Her fingers trembled, and she curled them tightly over her stomach. "There are reasons for what I did. They might seem unimportant to you, but they matter to me. I know it was wrong, but if I could explain, make you understand why—"

"No." Raoul raked his fingers through his hair. "I can't believe you'd do something like this. You knew I didn't want to be a father."

"You're not exactly a father, you're more like a..." Her voice trailed, and she bit her lip.

"A sperm donor?"

The words, spoken in a tone Julia had never heard from Raoul, made her flinch.

"I'm sorry," she whispered. "More than you know. But don't ask me to be sorry about this baby. I love it with all my heart."

He put his hand on the doorknob. "I need to think," he said. "If I stay, I will say something we'll both regret."

When Raoul had calmed down, he kept remembering the stricken expression on Julia's face. She loved the child she was carrying and thought she had good reasons for doing something so drastic to have it.

"Damn," he muttered, remembering how fragile she'd seemed.

She'd already said she was having trouble with the pregnancy. Could his reaction, however justified, upset her enough to threaten the baby? He might have not have chosen to become a father, but it was his child, and his responsibility to protect.

When he called Julia's office, he learned she'd left early. His nagging concern blossomed into worry, and Raoul hurried downstairs to catch a taxi. Darkness had fallen and the temperature was well below freezing, but he paid little attention.

Lights were shining in Julia's house and the scent of wood smoke drifted across the neighborhood. A peaceful setting, but there was nothing peaceful about the state of his mind. Raoul rang the bell, and after a minute the door opened.

Julia.

Her lovely eyes were red-rimmed, apparently from tears. Oddly, knowing she'd grieved over their argument eased his frustration. Whatever else, she wasn't a scheming marriage hunter. She had too much heart for that.

"All right," he said quietly. "Make me understand."

Chapter Four

Julia hadn't thought she had any tears left, but fresh ones welled in her eyes. She'd never meant to hurt Raoul or change his life, she'd just wanted a baby so badly she hadn't let herself think about how he'd feel.

If anything, she'd figured he wouldn't care, since so many men were casual about that kind of thing, claiming it was a woman's problem to keep from getting pregnant.

"Come in," she said, stepping back.

As they walked into the living room, Julia hurried over to the couch to collect the scattered tissues on the floor. She'd gone through an entire box of them, and it looked as if a snowstorm had hit the place.

"Don't worry about that," Raoul murmured.

"No, it'll only take a minute."

She wasn't even aware he'd gone, until he returned a couple of minutes later holding a glass. "You should be drinking milk, not fussing about picking up," he said gruffly. "Have you eaten dinner?"

"Some. Not much." Julia took the milk and sat on the edge of a chair. The gesture was kind and thoughtful, and something she didn't deserve after trapping him in the situation.

"How much at risk *is* your pregnancy?"

She sniffed. "The doctor is worried, but he says the baby is healthy, and should be fine if I can gain more weight. He's monitoring us closely."

"And how does he know the child is healthy?"

"From sonograms. I've had several, including one last week. It's...they told me it's a girl."

Raoul nodded. Julia was wearing a soft knit dress that molded her stomach, revealing what her heavy sweaters and loose skirts had concealed. She *was* small, though not as tiny as he'd feared. Her lithe, athletic figure accommodated the pregnancy more than some women's might.

Her daughter would be beautiful, like her, but he had trouble envisioning the child as a tangible reality. It seemed surreal in many ways, so very unexpected. Coming to Chicago he'd hoped to share something quite different with Julia than a baby.

"You said you had reasons for what you did. Help me to understand."

A soft sigh came from her, and she sipped her milk before answering. "Have you ever heard of endometriosis?" she asked.

"It's a feminine condition, is it not?"

"Yes." Julia wrinkled her nose. Describing endometriosis as a *feminine condition* sounded like an archaic understatement. "I've always had painful periods, but I grew up without a mother and I couldn't talk about it with my father. At least not much. He thought I was just being..." She stopped and shrugged.

"Being what?"

"A complainer. That I wasn't tough enough. I told you about him last night, remember? Mr. Three-Star General who doesn't put up with weaklings?"

Raoul's eyes darkened. "Truly, I do not like this father of yours, Julia. He did not deserve to have such a daughter."

It was a nice thing to say, especially after she'd tricked him into getting her pregnant.

"Anyway, I just learned to accept the pain as normal. Then in June I had some tests and the gynecologist diagnosed endometriosis. He told me that having a baby sooner, rather than later, might relieve the symptoms, only that isn't what I really cared about. You see…endometriosis can cause infertility."

Raoul muttered something in a language that sounded like Arabic. It sounded grim and angry, and she doubted she wanted to hear a translation.

Rather than look at him, Julia swallowed the last of her milk. She expected her stomach to revolt, but curiously, the nausea was temporarily gone. "I've always wanted children," she whispered, praying he would understand. "Then suddenly there wasn't any time and it seemed as if my life was out of my control."

"So you decided to take control by seducing a man and getting pregnant." His tone was calm again, but she knew he must be churning inside.

"I didn't actually need to seduce you," Julia said wryly. She felt terrible about what she'd done, but she believed in being honest. At the best of times she would have had trouble resisting Raoul. She'd smiled, shown her interest, and he'd pursued her with a single-minded intensity she'd never before experienced—not that she'd resisted, he was too perfect for her baby hopes.

From the reluctant smile tugging at Raoul's mouth, she knew he was thinking the same thing. "You fascinated me. I have known many women, but none like you."

"I'm not sure that's a compliment."

"Ah, but it is. You have a cool dignity, yet it cannot hide the fire beneath. I am right about the fire, yes? You did *feel* something when we were together?"

"If you're asking whether I faked my response in bed, certainly not," Julia snapped. "What kind of woman do you think I am?"

"That is what I'm trying to determine."

She gulped, reminded that Raoul was the injured party, not her. At the very least, he deserved to understand.

"Raoul, I was still in shock when I attended the conference," she said quietly. "It was just a few days after I'd gone to the doctor, and I couldn't think about anything else. I know that isn't a good excuse, but when we met it seemed like the answer to a prayer. You were strong and handsome and I knew you'd make a beautiful baby."

She wasn't sure, but she thought she saw a dull red creep under his skin at the compliment. It was sincere, Raoul was the most attractive man she'd ever met, with balanced, sensual features that weakened a woman's willpower. The way he walked, the heat in his eyes, everything about him was larger than life.

He cleared his throat. "In addition, I lived outside the country, so there was little chance I would discover what you'd done."

Julia set her glass down on the coffee table. She was

so confused. Her life had turned into a great big mess. And the worst part was wondering if she'd lose the baby and the pain would all be for nothing.

No. That isn't going to happen.

An inner determination made Julia lift her chin. If it was possible to make her little girl grow big and healthy by sheer force of will, then she'd make it happen. With that thought, she grabbed the glass again and climbed to her feet, muttering that she needed more milk.

"Julia…?"

Raoul followed Julia into the kitchen. For the sake of her pregnancy he was glad she was drinking milk, but he still didn't know how he felt about their affair. A woman's need to conceive and bear a child was a powerful biological force. His sisters would undoubtedly understand and defend Julia sight unseen.

He even understood. The pain in Julia's face had torn at him as well, so how could he condemn her?

I'm not ready to be a father, cried his alter ego, the part that wasn't happy over the consequences of their actions—her deceit, and his failure to use common sense.

Yet it was an accomplished fact.

His warring thoughts and emotions couldn't be ignored, but Raoul tried to set them aside. Ultimately, it didn't matter. It was his duty to ensure his child was safe and protected, which also meant protecting the child's mother.

"You should rest more," he muttered.

"I'm getting plenty of rest."

"Perhaps, but surely staying in bed for the next two months would be best for the child."

Julia shook her head. "The doctor doesn't think it's

necessary. Anyway, I don't want to take that much time from work. I'd rather be off after the baby comes.''

"If it's a question of money, I will—"

"No." She looked at him angrily. "I'm not taking a dime from you. And it isn't a question of money. As long as it doesn't hurt my pregnancy, I want to work.''

"It isn't that simple.''

"Look, I'm more sorry than I can say about what I did. But you don't have to worry. I'm not going to ask you for anything. You don't have to be a father to this baby, or think you have to support us. I make a good living at Kane Haley, Inc., and I'm very independent.''

Independent wasn't quite the word Raoul would have chosen. *Stubborn* and *unreasonable* were more appropriate, but he knew better than to say such things.

"I *am* the child's father.''

"You know what I mean.''

"Not really. Perhaps you should explain it, so we both understand.''

Plainly out of sorts, Julia poured another glass of milk and drank it before answering. She was so distracted she didn't realize a small amount of the white liquid rimmed her upper lip, but Raoul did. He wanted to lick it off himself, to taste her again, the way he'd tasted her in Washington. It was hardly an appropriate response, but nothing seemed to cool the heat in his blood—heat for Julia, even knowing how she'd used him.

"What I mean is…you don't have to be a daddy,'' she said after a long moment. "You don't have to spend time with the baby or claim her as your daughter. Nobody has to know. I'm sure Kane won't say anything unless we say something first, and I certainly won't talk about it.''

"It isn't that simple," Raoul said. "I am responsible for the child, whether you agree or not."

"That isn't what I wanted."

"What you wanted is meaningless now. I'm not happy with the circumstances, though I do understand why you felt it was so important. But you are carrying my daughter, Julia. I cannot turn my back on either of you. My conscience will not allow it."

"Your conscience? Raoul, this is the twenty-first century. I'm relieving you of responsibility. Do you think I'm incapable of caring for my own baby?"

"Of course not." The idea was ludicrous. Her strength was one of the things that continued to fascinate him. "But that does not mean I'm absolved of my duty."

She rolled her eyes in a uniquely American fashion. "That's incredibly old-fashioned."

"Perhaps, but it's the way I'm made. I have been thinking, and the only answer is for us to get married."

"The only...*what?*"

He'd obviously shocked her, yet it *was* the only solution to their situation. He couldn't take care of them properly outside of marriage, so marriage it must be. At least his mother would be pleased, Raoul thought with grim humor. To finally have one of her children wed and a grandchild arriving would delight Rihanna Oman greatly. Of course, he wouldn't reveal everything to his family—simply that they'd had an affair, and a child had resulted.

"We must get married, Julia."

Julia gulped and tried to think of a polite way to say no—a reasonable, calm explanation of the fact that she had no intention of marrying a man as autocratic and intense as Prince Raoul Oman. Only she'd have to be more diplomatic. She owed him that much.

"I will call my parents this evening. They'll want to come for the ceremony," Raoul added.

"No." She wasn't marrying him, and that was that.

"You do not wish to meet my parents?"

"*No*...I mean, yes, of course it would be nice to meet them. But we're not getting married."

One of his eyebrows shot upward. On some men it would have been an inquiry; on Raoul it was a statement of pure arrogance. In a single gesture he was informing her how foolishly and illogically he thought she was acting.

Emotional, maybe, but not foolish. *He* was the one who wasn't really thinking. If he was, he'd realize marrying her might end any hope of him fathering a son. She'd explained about her condition, that it might lead to infertility. Having a baby might relieve the symptoms, but it might not. Raoul claimed he wasn't a family man, but he could change his mind. Men did, particularly when it came to having sons. She had no intention of spending her life with someone who resented her or her daughter.

"This isn't Hasan," Julia said, trying not to lose her temper. "You can't order me to marry you. It's America, and women have babies by themselves all the time."

"Surely not if they have the choice of having a husband who will care for them."

Men.

"You may claim Hasan is liberated, but the evidence says otherwise," she murmured in a dry tone. "Pregnant or not, women don't need a man to 'care' for them. A hundred years ago, maybe, but not today."

"You deliberately misunderstand."

"What part of 'a husband who will care for them' didn't I understand?"

Raoul's face grew increasingly exasperated. "It was a figure of speech. Our marriage—"

"There isn't going to *be* a marriage."

Sighing, Julia rubbed the aching area in her lower back. While she might not have gained the healthiest number of pounds for a seven-months-pregnant woman, the shift of weight in her body made standing more and more uncomfortable.

"Please, Raoul, leave it alone. I appreciate your concern, but I need to do this on my own. We're too different to make a marriage work, and I'm too tired to argue about it any longer."

He frowned, his face unconvinced. "You must rest," he agreed. "We will talk more later. Do you need anything before I leave?"

"Just a good night's sleep."

"Very well." He stepped closer, gazing at her with a hungry energy. "This isn't finished, Julia. You are partly right about the differences between us, but not the right part. I have not chosen to be a father, but I *will* be this child's father, whether you understand it or not. Family responsibility is not something I can abandon."

Julia knew she ought to feel threatened, but she didn't.

From any other man she would have worried about a custody battle, or have been prepared to sign a waiver of responsibility. There'd probably have been demands for blood tests and discussions of legal agreements, and lots of money flowing into lawyer's pockets.

But not with Raoul.

Because *she* was part of that responsibility he felt, and he wouldn't hurt her. Even at a terrible cost to himself.

Somehow, that made her feel even worse.

"Such sad eyes," Raoul whispered. He cupped the side of her face, his thumb stroking gently across her cheek. "Don't think any longer about this tonight. *Grand-mère* once told me she didn't really know the dawn, until she had seen it rise over the desert. You see, when things are at their bleakest, beauty has its greatest chance to shine."

His warm breath washed across her skin as he leaned nearer, and Julia's eyes drifted closed. She could rail against him, recognize his character as being arrogant and controlling, but she didn't have any defense against the sensual half of his nature.

With the tip of his tongue he traced the contours of her lips, and Julia realized he was licking milk from her skin. She would have been embarrassed, thinking she'd looked silly, but the proof of Raoul's desire was pressed into the small bulge of her stomach. She moaned. He was the only man who'd ever made her feel this way, and temptation was just a breath away.

It was dangerous, delicious and utterly foolhardy. She couldn't let it continue.

She opened her mouth to protest, and Raoul took advantage of the moment to slip inside, joining them in a seamless kiss, their tongues dancing and mating in the silken pattern they'd discovered months before. And despite the confused throbbing in her body, she wondered if his skill in intimate kissing was something he'd inherited from the French side of his family.

He was good—too darned good—at it.

Thank heaven he hadn't asked her to marry him between kisses, because she couldn't think straight when he held her so closely. When Raoul finally broke free to drag breath into his lungs, she shuddered.

"I can't...make love," she managed to gasp. "The doctor...I haven't asked him about...that. And I'm sure the answer is no."

"It's all right."

Was it?

She'd made it sound as if she *would* have made love with him again, except for not knowing if it was safe. But baby or not, they didn't have a future. She'd never let a man control her again, and Raoul was too much a product of his royal upbringing. Besides, except for her brief lapse to get pregnant, she didn't believe in sex without commitment.

"Tell me one thing before I leave," Raoul said. "No matter what happens between us, you'll let my parents visit their grandchild."

"Of course they can visit. If they want to."

"They'll want to." The quiet certainty in his tone made Julia want to cry all over again. Crying was something she did too easily these days, though whether it was prompted by hormones or long-standing remorse, she didn't know.

"I really need to be alone now," she whispered.

"Of course. I will see you in the morning." He dropped a last kiss on her forehead and strode from the kitchen. The distinctive sound of the lock on the door came from the living room, then everything was silent again.

Shaking, Julia stumbled to the bedroom and curled up on the bed. She felt so tired. No matter what she'd said to Raoul, she hadn't slept well since leaving that June conference, too nagged by guilt and worry to relax. At least things were in the open now, and she wouldn't have to wonder if he would find out about the baby. The guilt was still present, but it had changed now that the worst had happened. Surely things could only get better.

"Right," she mumbled.

And Elvis Presley was still cutting records.

Still, Julia felt tension easing from her body, a tension that had been there so long she hadn't even realized it was her constant companion. She'd never done anything underhanded before, and deep down, she hadn't been able to escape the growing conviction that she'd harmed Raoul Oman in some unimaginable way.

With a concerned "meoooow," Muppet jumped up next to her, and curled close. He rested his whiskered face against the curve of her belly, seeming not to mind the thrumming vibration from the baby, who was kicking up a storm after being quiet all day.

Between his purr and the reassuring vigor of the infant in her womb, Julia yawned, her eyes closing sleepily.

Maybe tomorrow *would* be better.

At the very least, it couldn't get any worse than today had already been.

Raoul sat in his hotel suite late into the night, thinking about Julia and what she'd told him. His slow-burning anger had diminished and was shaded with regret. Their time together had been a lie, but at least she had shared a measure of his passion. He couldn't be that wrong about her.

In a way he admired Julia's determination. She'd been faced with a terrible decision and had taken action. And it was true that many men would not have cared if they fathered a child, as long as they didn't have responsibility for it. Such attitudes were foreign to him, just as treating women unkindly was something he could never do.

For all of Julia Parker's sophistication, beneath it she was a creature ruled by her heart—this he also admired. Emotion, rather than cool calculation, had propelled her into his bed.

I didn't actually need to seduce you.

Her wry comment rang in his head, and he shrugged. It was true enough. From the moment he'd seen Julia, he'd been determined to get her. The fact she'd smiled invitingly was irrelevant. And, in retrospect, he recognized the shock she'd spoken of, the emotional trauma of being told she might never bear a child.

He didn't like being used, but was it completely her fault? He was experienced with the ways of the world, had dealt with scheming women trying to gain something through a liaison, yet he'd made it absurdly easy for Julia to gain what she wanted.

He knew better than to let his body rule his head and common sense. Never, *ever,* had he made love without protection, even as an undisciplined youth, yet he'd broken his cardinal rule with Julia. What was even stranger, he still wanted her with a baffling intensity. Wanted her, despite the way she'd used him, despite his confused feelings about her and the child she carried.

The thoughts raced through Raoul's mind as he searched for some resolution. So when the phone rang, it was a welcome interruption to the cacophony going on inside his mind.

"Yes?"

"My son, I expected to hear from you sooner."

"Mother." A resigned smile curved Raoul's mouth. So much for the interruption being welcome. He loved her dearly, but with everything so unsettled, this wasn't a good time to speak with family.

"Is Chicago very cold?"

"It is January, Mother. In North America. Cold is to be expected."

"Yes, of course. It is lovely here, you know."

"I know."

He didn't need a reminder of the subtle beauty of his home. The stark magnificence of the desert, the ocean, the lush growth in the palace gardens. But Chicago was also filled with its own beauty and interesting features, including a raw energy that had always excited him.

"Son, you sound so…distant," his mother said hesitantly. "Is something wrong?"

Damnation.

If Julia had agreed to marry him, he would have called his parents and asked them to come for the wedding. But she hadn't. Even more, the daughter she carried was at risk. If he told his family, they might end up grieving a grandchild they would never be able to hold. He would have to wait until there was better news to share.

"I'm busy, that is all," Raoul murmured, ironically aware that he was perpetuating the lie Julia had started. "And tired. There is nothing wrong."

Rihanna Oman wasn't a woman who was easily swayed from her worries, but she must have sensed the finality in his response. They chatted for another few minutes, then he spoke with his father. There were a few business details that needed resolving, and he promised to review the financial records sent by e-mail earlier that day.

At length the conversation ended, and Raoul was able to be alone with his thoughts again.

He had no doubt he would eventually convince Julia to marry him. She loved the baby, and would surely recognize it was better for her daughter to have both a mother and a father. Until then, he would carry out his responsibilities at a distance.

It would be difficult, but not impossible.

"You look better," Maggie Steward said as she stepped into the elevator with Julia. "I was worried about you after yesterday."

Julia smiled. To her surprise, she'd slept better than she had in months. And she'd kept a full breakfast down, without the slightest hint of stomach trouble.

"I'm fine," she said, giving her standard answer. Whenever anyone asked, she was always fine. She didn't like people knowing too much about her problems and getting all sympathetic. Even Maggie and Sharon Waterton didn't know about the sleepless nights and constant worry over the baby's failure to gain enough weight.

Maggie regarded her doubtfully, but kept silent. The elevator dinged at the fourteenth floor, where Maggie got off, and Lauren and Rafe Mitchell got on.

"Hi guys," Julia said cheerfully. "How is married life treating you?"

The two smiled, flashed swift, almost goofy looks at each other, then plastered a professional demeanor on their faces once again. Rafe cleared his throat and looked down, while Lauren smiled.

"Fine," she said. She winked, glowing with the confidence that her new clothes and makeup and love had given her.

"I'm surprised you didn't go on a longer honeymoon," Julia murmured.

"Um...we will later," Rafe said. "Did you get Jack Waterton's report on the construction status for the child-care center?" he asked quickly.

"Yes, everything seems to be on schedule." The change in subject didn't surprise Julia. Lauren and Rafe were trying their best to keep things on a business level at the office, but everyone enjoyed seeing the way they looked at one another when they didn't think anyone was watching.

There wasn't time for more conversation because they'd arrived at the sixteenth floor. Rafe went one direction, while Julia and Lauren went the opposite. Julia was sure Rafe would have preferred spending the day alone at home with his wife, and a deep, wistful pang went through her.

What would it be like, to have that kind of love? Raoul had asked her to marry him, but it was out of his age-old code of honor, not from any softer emotions. Not that she *wanted* to be in love with him, Julia assured herself quickly. He was too arrogant and controlling—too much the kind of man she'd always ended up with in the past.

Lauren stopped to see Sharon Waterton and Julia nodded at both women, still lost in thought. Inevitably, she'd have to make an announcement about the baby, and it couldn't wait much longer. Her weekly visit to the obstetrician was in a couple of days; if she'd gained any weight, she'd let Maggie, Sharon and Lauren know it wasn't a secret any longer. They'd take care of spreading the news.

The door of her office stood open, jolting her from her reverie. A murmur of voices came from inside and she walked in, staring at the men behind her desk.

"No, it needs to be on the table," Raoul was saying to one of the building maintenance workers. "Higher, so she doesn't have to lean over."

"What's going on?" Julia demanded.

Raoul looked at her, offering one of his reserved smiles. "I am having a small refrigerator installed."

"Why?"

"So milk and other food will be available at all times," he explained, as if it were the most reasonable thing in the world.

"I don't need...there's a refrigerator in the lunchroom," she said through clenched teeth.

"You need one closer to encourage you to eat. I will keep it stocked with appropriate items. As I recall, strawberries were a particular favorite." His voice was velvety, low with a sexual intonation, and Julia fought a flush of embarrassment. Her love for strawberries had become a sensual game between them; she didn't appreciate the reminder in front of an audience.

"You aren't keeping it stocked with anything. That is, I want it out of here."

"Nonsense." Raoul handed the worker a large-denomination bill, and directed him to remove the carton. The man gathered the large box and packing materials, casting Julia a speculative glance. She glared, and he hurriedly departed.

She kicked the door closed behind her and glared again, this time at Raoul.

"Get it out of here."

He lifted a single eyebrow in his annoyingly arrogant style and she simmered with anger.

"I can take care of myself."

"You would deny me the opportunity to care for the child? There is little I can do while you carry the infant, except make things more convenient for you." He opened a large cooler next to her desk and began filling the small refrigerator with cartons of milk, containers of prepared fruit, and assorted other food products.

"Raoul, this isn't going to work," Julia said, trying to sound calm and reasonable when she felt anything *but* calm. "I can't be the only employee in the company who has a private refrigerator."

"Then I will buy one for each of the other offices," he replied. "Along with anything else I consider necessary for your well-being."

Julia gulped. How did she fight that kind of determination and financial resources?

"And I think we should announce your pregnancy immediately," Raoul added. "We will, of course, explain that I am the child's father."

We will, of course, explain that I am the child's father.

She stared, realizing he meant every word. Lord, how had everything gotten so out of control?

Chapter Five

A little lightheaded, Julia grabbed a chair and sank into it. Raoul couldn't mean it, not really. When he'd thought things over longer, he'd realize it was better not to say anything.

"That isn't such a good idea," she said as calmly as possible.

"It is the truth."

Truth.

Once again he was playing on her guilt. "I won't let you manipulate me, Raoul," she said with quiet desperation. "Nobody is ever doing that to me again."

Raoul adjusted the temperature setting and closed the door of the refrigerator, a frown creasing the space between his eyes. He wasn't manipulating her. There was nothing terrible about ensuring Julia had healthy food readily available to eat. She'd said the child was underweight, so it was important she have choices that tempted her appetite.

But as he looked at Julia, he saw an unfamiliar vulnerability in her face, a fear that he didn't understand. "I'm not manipulating you."

"Right. You and that imperious eyebrow of yours—you're trying to make me feel guilty."

His eyebrow?

What did his eyebrow have to do with anything?

"I already know you feel guilty, Julia. And I have no intention of making you feel worse. What's done is done, and we must move on."

"You don't expect me to believe that, do you?"

"I do not lie."

She crossed her arms over her abdomen and tapped her fingers on her elbows. The gesture emphasized the gentle swell of her belly, pulling the heavy knit sweater over the curve that held his daughter...*their* daughter. Her clothing had been cleverly selected to camouflage the pregnancy, but now that he knew the truth, he saw the evidence plainly.

"Why didn't you announce your pregnancy before?" he asked, knowing he needed to learn why she'd kept the secret for so long.

Julia's shoulders rose in a small shrug. "A few people know, but it's my business, not anyone else's."

"You are not proud of this child?"

Her hazel eyes blazed at him. "Of course I'm proud. That has nothing to do with it. But I can take care of myself and I didn't want anyone to think I needed help or special treatment or anything."

"A pregnant woman—"

"—isn't incapacitated," she snapped.

Raoul started to lift an eyebrow, then remembered what Julia had said about his eyebrow. He certainly wasn't imperious, but since it seemed to annoy her, he would be careful until she learned more of him.

"There is more to keeping silent, though, isn't there?"

Her shoulders rose in another shrug. "I wasn't…that is, I was having trouble with the pregnancy, and if anything happened to the baby I didn't want…you know."

Sympathy.

She didn't need to say the word, and Raoul fought the urge to gather her close, to soothe her fears away. He didn't want the intimacy and demands of marriage, wanted children even less, yet he would do his duty, and part of that duty was offering comfort.

"Your friends and co-workers would want to help you through a difficult experience," he murmured.

"But they wouldn't understand, not really. I'm the one who ran out of time." Julia's breath grew ragged, and she put her hands over her belly, protecting the mound with every ounce of her maternal instincts. "And I can't even do this part right."

She whispered the last part, probably unaware of having said it, and Raoul's eyes widened in sudden comprehension. Julia Parker was an honest woman, who'd done something desperate to have the child she'd always wanted. Now she might lose that child, and she was tearing herself apart.

Maybe he *should* talk with his family about this matter. Fatima, at least. As a doctor she could help advise him about the physical changes and stress Julia was going through.

"You aren't losing the baby," Raoul said firmly.

"No, of course not." But she replied so quickly, he knew she wasn't entirely convinced.

There was so much going on behind Julia's hazel eyes, he couldn't begin to sort it out. Guilt was easy to discern, but the other emotions were too complex.

Some of it had to do with her childhood, of that he was certain; she might have escaped her military father, but the scars were still there. Julia was strong, yet deep down, she struggled with a fear that she wasn't quite strong enough.

"When do you see the doctor?" he asked.

"Friday. I thought if he says I've gained some weight, I'd let people know."

Raoul started to ask if he could go with her to the doctor since he was the baby's father, then stopped. She accused him of manipulating her, and he didn't want to upset her further.

"That sounds excellent," he said easily. "As for the refrigerator, Julia, it is a small thing. I would truly like you to accept it."

She looked mulish again, but that was fine. Anything was better than seeing her desolate expression.

"When the child is born, you can offer it to another co-worker who is expecting," he added. "Would this be acceptable to your stubborn independence?"

"I...oh, all right. But I don't want you filling it up with milk and food," Julia ordered. "I can feed myself."

Raoul smiled, neither agreeing or disagreeing. He would continue to supply the small refrigeration unit with anything he thought might tempt her appetite.

"I have a meeting now," he said. "But will you have lunch with me today?"

"No."

"Julia," he chided, "I dislike reminding you, but you owe me a lunch. We never ate yesterday."

She gave him a level look. "That was yesterday. Besides, I'm supposed to have lunch with Sharon Waterton."

"Then we will have dinner together." Julia opened her mouth to protest, but Raoul had already walked out of the office.

Wretched man.

He might claim he wasn't trying to manipulate her, but that was exactly what he doing. Lunch, refrigerator, milk, *strawberries*...of all the nerve. He'd actually reminded her about strawberries in front of a complete stranger. Raoul Oman didn't play fair, he played to win. Of course, it *was* his baby, she reminded herself grudgingly. But that didn't mean she was going to lunch or dinner or anything else with him.

Sighing, she got up and slid behind her desk. After a few minutes examining her weekly planner, she glanced at the refrigerator quietly humming away in the corner of the office. Incredibly, she was hungry again, and the darned thing was just sitting there, full of healthy stuff for the baby.

Inching her chair over, she opened the door and gazed inside—everything from milk and fruit to rice pudding and a fat chicken salad sandwich, wrapped in halves, with olives and pickles. She hadn't been subject to cravings during her pregnancy, but suddenly that sandwich looked like manna from heaven.

The baby kicked.

"You want the pickles and olives, is that it, sweetheart?"

The baby gave her another enthusiastic kick, and she smiled.

"All right, pickles and olives it is."

Julia pulled out half the sandwich, along with milk and rice pudding, and proceeded to polish them off. It was an unusual second breakfast, but it settled well on her stomach. She concentrated on the work piled on her desk, only thinking about Raoul every *other* minute, mostly when she sipped milk or felt the baby move.

For the first time in weeks, she was feeling hopeful. She was finally able to eat, the baby was active, and Raoul couldn't really want to marry her. He might have proposed in a fit of overdeveloped responsibility, but he'd lose interest after a while.

She'd heard nothing turned a dedicated bachelor off more than a pregnant woman, so maybe she should make her pregnancy more obvious—right away, even before seeing the doctor. And there were plenty of clothing stores close by. She'd just cancel lunch with Sharon and go shopping for maternity dresses that emphasized her expanding tummy.

If that didn't push Raoul away, nothing would.

Smiling to herself, Julia called Sharon Waterton. "Hi, it's Julia. I need to cancel lunch."

"Is something wrong?" Sharon asked, concern lacing her voice.

"No, but I want to shop for maternity clothing, and I know you've got plenty, so—"

"I'd love to go with you," Sharon said. "I'll look for a slinky maternity nightgown so I can turn Jack into a drooling idiot."

"Do you need a slinky nightgown for that?"

"No, but it's fun seeing how high I can hike up his blood pressure."

"You're all heart. I'll see you at one."

Julia said goodbye and replaced the receiver. It was time she made an announcement about the baby, though she suspected most everyone knew already. Her tummy wasn't *that* small, and people gossiped, even in a company like Kane Haley, Inc.

She'd just wear one of the new maternity dresses back to the office. As the old saying went, a picture was worth a million words, and her expanding stomach should be able to speak for itself.

Late that afternoon Raoul watched Julia standing in the corridor, talking with Maggie Steward. He couldn't resist a smile. Her heavy sweater and skirt were gone, replaced by a chic silk dress that clung to the curves of her body—especially her stomach. Dressed in such a manner, no one could doubt she was with child.

If this was how she'd chosen to announce her approaching motherhood, then it was certainly effective. What he didn't understand was why she'd decided not to wait until after her doctor's appointment.

Andy Huffman, head of the accounting department, rolled up in his wheelchair. "Julia, I just heard you're expecting," he exclaimed jovially. "Congratulations, young lady. You'll be a fine mother."

Julia's cheeks reddened a tiny bit. "Thank you. I'm very happy."

"Somebody mentioned the baby is small," Andy murmured. In the short time Raoul had been at the company, he'd always seen a smile on the older man's face, but now he looked worried. "Do you have anyone to help you?"

For a fraction of an instant, Julia's head lifted and she locked gazes with Raoul. His eyebrow instantly shot upward, though he tried to control the gesture.

"I'm fine," she said tensely.

"But it must be difficult to...well...be alone at a time like this."

She swallowed visibly. "Andy, you're sweet to be

concerned, but I'll be all right.'' Turning, she hurried away.

Raoul gritted his teeth, furious that Julia had avoided discussing the father of her baby. She wasn't alone now, and she wouldn't ever have *been* alone if she'd just told him. Of course, the pregnancy shouldn't have happened in the first place, but as he'd told her, it was done and over and he was trying to move beyond her deception.

Moreover, he wouldn't accomplish anything by arguing with her. They weren't children, they could come to a mutually acceptable agreement. He should calm down, then speak with her. Yet, despite his reasonable thoughts, Raoul's feet carried him to the door of Julia's office less than an hour later.

He rapped on the door, and when there wasn't an answer, he tried the knob.

Locked.

Beneath his breath, Raoul uttered a curse that rarely passed his lips.

Just then Sharon Waterton walked past, obviously leaving for the day. ''I think Julia's gone home,'' she said. ''Is there something I can do for you, Mr. Oman?''

Sharon had a sweet, almost innocent face, and Raoul hoped she didn't speak enough French to understand his earlier profanity. ''Thank you, Mrs. Waterton. I will arrange a meeting with Ms. Parker…tomorrow.''

''I didn't realize you were working together. Your departments aren't that closely connected.''

Sharon's eyes were utterly guileless, which just made him angrier. He should not be required to pretend a business association with the woman carrying his child. Everyone should know about this relationship with Julia, so they would not be surprised by his attentiveness to her. There would be questions and talk enough without more secrets complicating matters.

"Have a good evening, ma'am," he said formally, avoiding the subtle question she'd posed.

His car had been delivered by the Mercedes dealership, so Raoul drove immediately to Julia's house and knocked sharply on the door. "Julia?" he called loudly.

Inside Julia groaned.

Why couldn't Raoul leave her alone?

The knocking and calling continued until she pulled a satin robe around her. She'd been getting ready for a shower, but she doubted he'd be willing to wait while she dressed again. The only time Raoul Oman was patient was when he was controlling the outcome...like in bed with a woman.

"What?" she demanded, opening the door a crack.

"We need to talk."

"We talked last night."

"Obviously not enough."

He pushed past her, invading her home the way he'd done each of the previous two days. "What is it now?" she asked, tightening the sash of her robe—she was wearing only underwear beneath, and it made her nervous. "You know perfectly well that I'm not going to dinner with you, if that's what you're steamed about. Besides, I've already eaten, and have no intention of going out again."

"I am steamed, as you put it, that you did not tell Andy Huffman I am the child's father." Raoul's dark eyes blazed at her. "You dishonor me by allowing everyone to think I would abandon my responsibilities."

"I'm not dishonoring you," Julia said helplessly. "You didn't choose to be in this situation and I'm trying to protect your privacy. You must see that it's less complicated that way...much better all around for everyone."

"I did not ask you to keep it private. I have every intention of claiming the child as my own."

He was absolutely serious, and Julia sank onto the couch. She'd hoped he would think things over and decide he'd gotten off lightly, but she should have known better. Raoul had a rigid code of honor; he wouldn't give it up to save his life. He'd fathered a child, and regardless of his personal feelings on the matter, he considered himself duty-bound to take care of them. *Both* of them.

But what kind of father could Raoul be? He kept calling her little girl "the child." As though the baby was simply an object. Julia knew all about having a father who resented the responsibility of being a parent, and the pain of never quite being loved. She'd grown up in that kind of household and didn't want the same for her daughter.

"Julia," Raoul said more gently as he sat next to her. "This is difficult for both of us. Surely we can reach an understanding."

Understanding?

Sure. Right. And she believed in the tooth fairy.

Oh *why* hadn't she seriously considered a sperm bank? Men donating sperm had signed away all parental claims, they were faceless, nameless baby makers. They weren't tangled up in duty and honor and deception. Worst of all, she felt a traitorous need to curl up to Raoul and cuddle. It was definitely a weakness, because she doubted he was much good at cuddling. And since cuddling led to other things—like hot sex and more regrets—it wasn't smart to think about. She had enough regrets for one lifetime.

"I want you to reconsider what I proposed last night," he murmured.

Her head shook in automatic denial. "It would never work. People who don't love each other shouldn't get married."

She half expected him to say that people who didn't love each other shouldn't be having children, either, but he didn't. Maybe because arranged marriages were more common in his part of the world, or maybe because she'd claimed he was trying to make her feel guilty and he didn't want to prove her right.

"Why are you so convinced it wouldn't work between us?" Raoul asked after a long moment. He brushed her cheek with his hand, a gesture that was both gentle and enticing. "You are so very lovely. Having you in my bed each night would give me great pleasure."

Julia found herself swaying toward his warmth and stiffened her spine; Raoul Oman couldn't get around her with flattery or seduction. She was smarter than that.

"It just wouldn't," she said, though not as firmly as she'd have liked. "The truth is, we hardly know each other. We're practically strangers."

An arrogantly confident expression filled Raoul's face. "We know the important things. We are compatible sexually and have similar interests."

"Men," she muttered darkly. "Sex isn't everything."

"I did not say it was everything. We have many important similarities."

Shaking her head, she scooted sideways on the couch, trying to keep the edges of her robe together. It was hard to think with him so close. While she might protest the importance of making love, it had been the only real part of their relationship—a passion so fierce it had scared her.

"No. You *don't* know me," Julia said. "We're from different parts of the world, with different family backgrounds and educations. But more than anything else, I'm not the kind of woman you normally date."

"Oh?"

His eyebrow shot upward in his habitual style of inquiry, and Julia regarded him wryly. She wasn't terribly perceptive about men, but she'd learned a few things about Raoul during their time together. And one of those things was that he didn't date women who wanted more than a sophisticated affair—no permanent sort of women with booties and diapers on their minds.

She took a deep breath.

"Tell me something. If I'd said I wanted a baby at any time when we were together in Washington, would I have ever seen you again?"

"That's irrelevant now," Raoul said, though he looked uncomfortable.

"No, it isn't," she whispered.

His passionate feelings had changed, despite what he claimed. He saw her differently, no longer using the endearments that came so naturally to him. She ought to be grateful, but instead she missed the velvet heat of his voice when he wooed her in French.

"I'm not the kind of woman who falls in bed with a man just five hours after meeting him. Well…not usually," she added with her inherent honesty, because she *had* fallen into bed with him the night they'd met.

"If I'd been myself, you would have lost interest after five minutes. And pretty soon I'll be huge and irritable with swollen ankles...even more different from what I was in Washington."

"I do not care about these things," he said, attacking the easiest part of her speech. "You will be lovely regardless."

"The point is, I'm pregnant. I'm not slim or graceful or any of the things men want in a lover."

Raoul took a deep breath. Julia's eyes swirled with emotions, but he could sort out only a few. One of them was doubt...doubt that he desired her.

"You think I won't want you because of the baby."

"You don't want me now, not if you're honest with yourself."

Raoul's eyes widened. She believed it, believed he no longer desired her. "We kissed last night, remember? I would have taken you to bed if you'd allowed it."

"That was last night." Julia's gaze shifted away and she flicked the tip of her tongue over her lips. His body hardened watching her, his breath coming more harshly.

"And what has changed in the past day?"

"You can't ignore that I'm pregnant, for one thing. And I know you don't feel the same, you don't..." Her words trailed and she bit her lip.

"Don't what?"

"Nothing."

It wasn't nothing. He knew that expression. From one of his sisters it said he'd missed some vital information, clear only to the female mind. Though of course, the female mind was intriguing in the way it worked, and he wouldn't change it, even if he had the power.

"Perhaps," Raoul whispered, leaning closer to Julia, "we should test this attraction to see whether it still exists."

"Raoul, don't," she pleaded. "It's more than my body changing because of the baby. I've never been like that...the way I acted when we were together. It was just a fluke for me to respond so much. I'm sure it wouldn't happen again."

He smiled. For an intelligent woman, Julia didn't know herself at all. Yet he found her lack of confidence rather endearing. If he had to become a family man, there were worse fates than having Julia Parker in his future; she would keep things most interesting.

"Besides, I meant it about not sleeping around," she added.

"I won't take you to bed," he said, slipping his fingers through her silky hair. He drew a deep breath, filling his senses with her unique fragrance. "You are right not to risk the child's well-being, but we should see if you are correct about my desire for you."

A sad, almost despairing look filled her gold eyes, but he could only deal with one problem at a time. The idea that he'd lost interest was both baffling and laughable. He disliked the way he'd been used, yet it had done nothing to cool his need for her. If anything he wanted her more than ever.

"The first thing you need to understand," Raoul said, casually tugging on the tie holding her robe together. "Is that men from Hasan appreciate women who are warm and round to hold. We do not share your countrymen's blind concept of beauty."

Julia was holding perfectly still, barely breathing. He

hesitated, waiting for a refusal before easing the edges
of the garment over her shoulders. His groin burned at
the sight of her body, desire slamming him so hard he
could hardly breathe. She was lovelier than ever, beyond the dreams that had haunted his sleep since they
were last together. Lace panties were taut across her
rounding stomach. Her pale breasts strained against a
transparent silk bra, fuller than before, the lush mounds
crowned by tips darkened to a dusky rose.

Memories cascaded through him, memories of how
it felt to have her hard nipple in his mouth, the soft
moans and eager sounds she made as he filled her. She
was the only woman he'd ever made love to unpro-
tected, and the sensation of her soft, clinging heat was
seared into his senses.

"Julia..." he groaned, hands moving down until he
could gather the generous bounty into his palms.

The pulse jumped at the base of her throat and Raoul
kissed the spot while his thumbs rotated, exciting those
rose nipples with every ounce of skill at his command.

"So beautiful," he said, low and guttural. "So perfect. How could I not want you?"

Beset with sensations, Julia trembled and fought the
temptation to meet caress with caress, and kiss with
kiss. She couldn't, *shouldn't* encourage him, no matter
how much she wanted it. He didn't love her or want a
child with her.

Sometimes at night she'd dreamt Raoul was there,
holding her, saying all the things she longed to hear
from a man. But in the morning the dream faded, because Sheik Oman was entirely the *wrong* man. He
ordered, rather than asked, and controlled, rather than
compromised. Marrying him would be the biggest mistake of her life.

But oh…it felt so nice, being held like this again, to be reminded of being a woman. Her nipples were more sensitive from pregnancy, and when he suckled one of the hard points through her bra, her body nearly shot off the couch. She threaded her fingers through his black hair, holding him to her. His lips moved to her other breast, laving it with an attentive tongue. She'd forgotten how good he was, how generous in bed, though he controlled the outcome.

"So sweet," he groaned, shuddering against her.

Without conscious thought Julia slid down until she was lying prone on the cushions, Raoul slowly devouring her with his kisses. Her head was arched over his forearm, and nothing seemed real but the hard pressure of his mouth and body.

"Feel me," Raoul muttered into her mouth. "Touch the proof of my desire. It is not something I can hide— surely you know this much about men." He caught her unresisting hand and drew it down over his stomach, and still lower, where the hardness of his arousal pressed into her thigh.

As if in protest to her mother's weakness, the baby suddenly kicked, shattering the sensual haze enveloping them both.

Raoul drew back, startled. "What was that?"

Julia took several breaths and shook her head to clear it. "The baby…she kicked."

"The child did that?"

The child.

He wanted to take her to bed, but the baby she carried had no real connection to him beyond an unwelcome responsibility. Her daughter was just "the child" to Raoul. Julia wanted to think it was his formality, a man speaking a language foreign to him, but she didn't believe it.

Blinking away tears, she put her hands on his shoulders and gave him a good hard push. "Yes," she hissed. "The *child* kicks a lot—babies do that. So now you've proven your point that we're still sexually compatible, please leave."

"Julia—"

"Go away."

He was clearly perplexed about her reaction, which angered her even more.

"We aren't getting married, and that's that. So just leave me alone."

"You must be reasonable."

"You be reasonable. If nothing else, think about this—you come from a royal family that needs male heirs, and I'm having trouble carrying this baby. This little *girl.* And I may never have another child." Julia's ravaged face told Raoul how much she hated voicing her fears aloud.

"Julia, don't." He couldn't bear for her to say more, to hurt herself further. "That isn't something you should worry about."

Her head shook. "No. I don't care what you say about not wanting to marry and have children. Someday you'll want a son, and I probably won't be able to give it to you."

Raoul sighed and rocked back on his heels. He'd tried to prove he found her more attractive than ever, and he'd succeeded. But he had a strange conviction that while he'd won the battle, he might have lost the war.

Chapter Six

Two weeks later Raoul was no closer to understanding Julia than the night she'd ordered him out of her house.

Truly, women were impossible creatures. Yet, deep in his heart, Raoul knew he'd missed something important.

But what?

He had a disturbing idea that he'd wasted much of his life with companions who challenged neither his mind nor his spirit. Julia was a complete unknown, he wasn't prepared to deal with her on any level.

His one consolation was seeing her blossom with health. The baby was growing quickly and through office gossip he learned the obstetrician was pleased with the child's progress. He'd also heard that her co-workers, Sharon Waterton and Lauren Mitchell, were planning a baby shower as a surprise...an event he planned to attend, if only for the chance to speak with her.

Early the following Wednesday morning Raoul

stepped from Julia's office, the usual ice chest in hand, and found her outside scowling at him.

"I knew you had to be coming in early, or staying late to fill up the refrigerator. I told you I didn't want you to bring food for me."

"It is nothing."

Her sigh sounded less exasperated than resigned. "All right, but please don't make it obvious to everyone."

"I have *been* discreet," he said, bitterness creeping into his tone, though he tried to control it.

Julia's lashes swept down, concealing her eyes. "Yes, you have. Thank you."

Raoul told himself to be patient. That last night at her house he'd again broached the subject of marriage, without giving her enough time and space to consider the advantages. He should have waited, but her reluctance to acknowledge him as the baby's father had infuriated him, overriding his better judgment. This time, he would be more careful.

The building was quiet, they were the only ones present at such an early hour. Nevertheless, Raoul glanced up and down the corridor to ensure they had privacy.

"We haven't resolved anything," he said quietly. "You did not even tell me how your doctor's visits went. I had to find out through employees discussing the matter—the 'grapevine' I believe it's called. I do not enjoy having to learn of you from idle gossip."

She swallowed and looked at him helplessly.

"Take another week," Raoul said, "to decide how to tell your co-workers and friends about our relationship. But you must tell them, Julia. We cannot go on this way."

"Raoul, that isn't—"

"Please," he murmured, wanting to convince her, rather than insist. Her accusation that he manipulated her was too fresh for comfort. "It is important to me. When Mr. Huffman talked about you being alone, I felt…disgrace." It was a difficult thing to admit and his free hand clenched into a fist on his thigh.

"There isn't any need for that. You aren't expected to do anything."

"*I* expect it."

For a long moment he couldn't read anything in her sad face, then she nodded. "All right. I'll work something out."

"Is it so terrible, having me in your life again?" he asked, wanting to understand. "I'm not a cruel man. I would give you and the child anything you wanted. If you question my fidelity, I promise you'd never have reason to doubt me. Marriage vows are sacred in my family."

Unaccountably, Raoul saw tears fill her golden hazel eyes, the sadness growing in her expression, rather than diminishing. "Responsibility and duty aren't enough for a marriage to work. And they aren't enough to make a father. I know," she whispered.

He wanted to hold her and kiss the tears away, but he knew she'd deny his right to such an action. Ultimately, he didn't have any rights with Julia and the uncertainty of such a position was maddening. Kane kept urging him to take legal action, but he had no intention of distressing her with a lawsuit. His only recourse was to have faith in her intelligence and reason.

Early that evening, Raoul reluctantly dialed the palace in Hasan, knowing he could no longer delay telling his family the news. It was morning in Hasan, and his father's manservant answered the call. Raoul asked if his sister, Fatima, was available. She was, and some of his uneasiness turned to relief. Of his whole family, Fatima was the most reasonable. She had a scientist's mind and wasn't usually prone to emotional outbursts.

"Raoul…darling. Mother will be disappointed, she is at her charity foundation," Fatima said in greeting. "But of course, you know she always goes to the foundation this time of the morning, and that father will be in conference with grandfather."

"Yes." He smiled, his first real smile in the past two weeks. "I have something to tell you."

"Oh?"

"I…do you remember me telling you about Julia Parker, the woman I met last June?"

"Yes, very well. You've never discussed one of your women before." His sister's voice had sharpened with interest.

Unaccountably, Raoul was annoyed. "She isn't one of 'my women,' as you put it." He didn't want his family to think Julia was one of the women he'd been casually connected with over the years, because she wasn't. From the very beginning she'd been different, though he'd tried not to see it.

There was a short silence. "I remember you spoke warmly of Ms. Parker. She sounded most engaging."

Raoul sighed. He'd practically been obsessed with Julia after returning to Hasan, which was why he'd finally talked about her with Fatima. He could hardly speak of a woman with his mother or father; they would have been delighted to hear of his preoccupation with Julia, and hopeful of a permanent commitment. The fact she was an American wouldn't have mattered, not with the possibility of grandchildren from the union.

"Raoul?" his sister prompted.

"Fatima, Julia is pregnant." This time the silence stretched on and on, until he sighed again. "I am the father," he added.

"I can't believe…she hid this from you?"

Fatima sounded outraged, and Raoul clenched the telephone receiver in his hand. He'd decided not to reveal Julia's deception, but it wasn't to save his pride. He wanted them to embrace her as part of the family, and knowing she'd deliberately tricked him would make it more difficult.

"Julia knew how I felt about marriage and children. She thought I wouldn't want to know of the baby." It wasn't a lie, just not the complete truth.

"Then she doesn't understand you."

He agreed, but this wasn't the time to say it aloud. "She has not always known honorable men, Fatima. She's been hurt and believed I would be like the others."

"When are you getting married?"

Raoul winced. "I haven't convinced her—she's very independent. Truly American in every way."

"You finally propose marriage and the answer is no?" Fatima began laughing and between her hearty chuckles he tapped his fingers on the arm of the chair. "I want to meet this strong-willed American," his sister announced. "She must be delightful."

"Delightful? She refuses to marry me," he said, exasperated. "Then she convinced herself that I didn't want her because she's large with child."

"Do you?"

A vision of Julia's ripe curves rose before his mind's

eye and he fought the usual tightening in his groin when he thought of her. "Yes," he said huskily. "I want her very much."

"Do you love her?"

"Love has nothing to do with this. She's carrying the child I fathered, she should become my wife."

"How romantic."

Raoul glared at the opposite wall. He'd suspected his sisters would side with Julia. Women being women, they'd probably take her side even if they knew the truth. "She has agreed to allow Mother and Father to visit the child when it is born. I am certain she'll eventually agree we should marry."

"The *child?*" his sister asked in an odd tone. "You've said that twice now."

"What has that to do with anything?"

"Nothing...it just isn't very personal."

He scowled. "I fathered the child, that's personal enough. Tell Mother and Father about what is happening, but try to keep them in Hasan. I have enough problems without their interference. Tell them I'll call when I have some news."

After saying goodbye, Raoul frowned thoughtfully, trying to decide whether things had fallen apart between him and Julia. Fatima's comments niggled at the back of his mind, as if the answer lingered, waiting to be found in the midst of things said, and not said.

The problem was, he needed to spend time with Julia to discover any real answers, and she'd gone out of her way to avoid him. He'd wanted to demonstrate he wasn't manipulative, as she'd claimed, but enough was enough.

Julia walked out of the office building and drew a breath of cold air, reveling in the blue January sky. She was taking the afternoon off from work to go shopping now that the baby was doing so well.

"Hello, Julia."

Raoul's low voice didn't even startle her, and she watched as he climbed out of the sleek silver Mercedes sitting by the curb. She was so mixed up about him. A part of her knew he was a controlling, overbearing man who shouldn't be a part of her daughter's life. But the other part—the one that missed his French endearments and the special warmth in his dark eyes—wondered if she was overlooking something.

"Where are you going?" he murmured.

"Shopping."

"Ah…you will need a strong arm then. Allow me to escort you." He gestured toward the Mercedes and waited with a challenging smile on his face.

So much for a peaceful day of shopping in the nearby stores. She wouldn't be able to buy anything, because Raoul would be stubborn and interfere, but she could look and go back later if there was anything she particularly wanted.

As they drove to a shopping area she suggested, Raoul chatted about people at the office and his observations of Chicago. It was warm in the car and Julia let down some of her guard. When he wanted to be, Raoul Oman was a charming companion, both funny and intelligent. Within a few minutes he had her laughing over a subtle confrontation of wills he'd observed between Kane Haley and Maggie Steward.

"Mrs. Steward is an excellent administrative assistant," Raoul said. "Kane is fortunate to have her."

"Yes, he is," Julia agreed, though she wasn't always sure Kane *knew* how lucky he was. There were few people more loyal to Kane than Maggie, but she was a bit shy and insecure, which made it hard for people to really see her.

Raoul pulled into a parking lot and strode around to the passenger's side to help Julia from the Mercedes. She gratefully accepted—the baby had grown so quickly she was more awkward than normal.

Once inside the small, upscale shopping mall, Julia shrugged out of her coat, breathing a sigh of relief.

"You'll get chilled," Raoul protested.

"You've never been pregnant," she muttered without thinking. "I'm always hot these days—it's like I have a little furnace burning inside me."

"Hmm." He took her coat and tucked it over his arm, along with his overcoat. "Are you very uncomfortable with the kicking and everything?"

Julia couldn't tell if he was really interested, or just playing his part as a responsible father of *the child*. Lord, she hated it when he said that. She'd tried believing it didn't mean anything, but there was too much doubt...and too much potential for her daughter to be hurt.

And one thing was certain, Raoul wasn't going away. He would do his duty, no matter the cost.

"I'm fine," she said. "It might be uncomfortable, but every time she kicks, it reminds me she's alive and healthy. For a while the kicking was the only thing getting me through the day."

"What did the doctor say about the child's weight?"

Julia let out a breath and tried not to roll her eyes. "Approaching low normal. Another week or so and we should be on schedule. I've been eating constantly and sleeping better, which helps."

"I am glad."

The fifth store they visited was filled with toys and Swedish baby furniture. With delight, Julia touched a mobile hanging above one of the cribs. The pieces were made of hand-painted wood, intricately fitted to look like long-limbed cats, chasing each other's tails through the air.

"You like this? I'll have it wrapped for you." Raoul motioned to a clerk and Julia schooled her expression.

"It's nice, but I'm just looking," she said, stepping away from both the mobile and crib. Raoul wanted to buy everything she looked at.

The saleswoman appeared, smiling obsequiously. "When is your due date, ma'am?"

"In about six weeks."

"Are you looking for anything in particular?"

Julia shook her head. "To be honest, I haven't gotten anything yet. I've been...waiting."

"Waiting?" The other woman seemed curious, but before she could say anything else Raoul cleared his throat.

"We are just looking," he said firmly. "That will be all."

Most people would have quailed under the tone of Raoul's voice, and the saleswoman was no exception. "Of course, sir. I'll be around if you need me."

Julia wanted to be annoyed at his interference, but he *had* saved her from an explanation. She didn't want to say anything about her difficult pregnancy, or her early fears that she might never get to use any clothes or toys she got for the baby.

"Does everyone do what you tell them?" she asked as they strolled from the shop and into another. "A member of the royal family speaks and the masses listen?"

"Almost everyone, except a certain American woman who won't listen to reason," Raoul replied, humor gleaming in his dark eyes. "She is very stubborn."

"Maybe she's just smart."

"She *is* smart…and beautiful. Even when she's being completely obstinate."

Julia smiled and put her hand on her stomach. The baby was doing a lazy stretch and dive. It was an extraordinary sensation, redolent with peace and well-being.

"May I touch you?" Raoul asked, watching the movements beneath her fingers.

More than anything Julia wanted someone to share moments like this with, but she didn't think Raoul was the right someone. *It's his baby,* her conscience scolded. Her hesitation brought a thoughtful frown to his face.

"What is it, Julia? I've asked what troubles you about involving me in the child's life, but you haven't given me answers that make sense."

"Don't you see?" she asked, blinking tears from her eyes. "It isn't your fault—you never wanted to be a father—but you can't even say 'my baby' or 'our daughter.' She's just 'the child' to you. She'll be a thinking, feeling little girl who will see her friends with adoring daddies and wonder why there's a wall between you and her. And trust me, she'll blame herself."

She'll blame herself.

All at once Raoul saw a younger Julia in his mind's eye. A girl sweet and energetic, loving with her whole heart, and certain she'd failed her father in some terrible way.

"I'm not like him," he said harshly, appalled she would think he would treat a child so unkindly.

A stillness came over Julia's face. "Like who?"

"Your father."

"This isn't about him."

"It is. You think I would be like that, hurting the…our daughter."

"You won't mean to, but you'll hurt her just the same. Children know the difference between duty and love, and you don't love her. After what I did, I don't think you can. You'll blame us both for changing your life."

Raoul cursed into his mind, understanding more than she'd said. Julia hadn't forgiven herself for tricking him, so she didn't believe he could, either. It was true he'd resisted marrying and becoming a father, but that didn't mean he couldn't change. She had been his sweetest of lovers, and would soon bear his child. If he had any chance of happiness with a woman, it was with Julia.

"Julia," he whispered. They were in a secluded corner of the shop and he cupped her cheek in his hand. She was lovely, all pink and gold, the colors of his desert home at sunrise. "My feelings for you have not changed. I burn for you in a way I've never burned for a woman."

"You have changed."

"You cannot know that."

"I do." She lifted her eyes, and Raoul ached with the pain in them. "French endearments are a natural part of expressing yourself with people you care about, and you haven't uttered a single French word to me since you learned of the baby."

"You ordered me *not* to."

"Since when did you ever take orders?" she retorted.

Raoul sighed. "Not often, but I did not mean to give you doubt. I admit the baby...*our* baby, was a shock. What I thought was real about our affair, wasn't. You've refused to let me close and denied my right to help you. These are not things a man finds easy to handle, and I have been distracted."

"The passion was real," she whispered. "Washington was real. But you scared me. You're so intense, and even in bed you had to be in control."

"No, I...." With an effort Raoul swallowed the remainder of his denial.

Was it true?

He might protest the influence of his royal upbringing, but could he, in complete honesty, deny he was accustomed to things being done his way? Was it so hard to believe he'd become arrogant and controlling, exactly the way Julia had claimed? The thought was distasteful. His father had said that power didn't make you a man, and the best ruler was one who served his people more than they served him. But that lesson had seemed important only for his older brother, since he was the heir who would one day rule Hasan.

Now Raoul realized his father's lesson had also been meant in a larger way. A man could have his pride, but it meant nothing if he took pride from another.

"Julia," he said softly. "I have much to think about. You want the best for our daughter, as do I. But you are right that I have trouble seeing her as a real person—perhaps because I've never spent much time with children."

"So what's the answer?"

"This, to start." Raoul lifted Julia's hand from her

stomach, and placed his own over the supple mound that protected his child. The vigorous strength of the baby sent a curious mix of emotions through him. Pride. Relief at the healthy movements…awe of a woman's body in a way he'd never felt before.

"Raoul?"

"Teach me," he whispered. "*That* is the answer. Teach me the love you have for this child. Help me to be the father you want for her. I swear by all I hold holy, I will not disappoint you."

Julia held her breath, wanting to believe Raoul. He was a decent man. She'd known that from the beginning, or else she would never have gotten into bed with him. But could he change that much? Enough to be a real father?

Maybe. Maybe not.

But he wasn't going away, so it was her only hope.

Chapter Seven

The next afternoon Julia sat in her office, staring at the company phone list. She didn't really need the list—Raoul's number had been added the day he arrived, and she knew it by heart from looking at it so often.

But that didn't make it easier to dial.

He'd taken a step the day before.

Teach me the love you have for this child. Help me to be the father you want for her. I swear by all I hold holy, I will not disappoint you.

His request and promise had shaken her deeply. From the depths of her heart she wanted to believe him.

Now it was her turn to take a step, but she was still frightened, worried what it might mean for the baby nestled under her heart. She'd never expected Raoul to see how her childhood was influencing the decisions she was making now. This wasn't about her father, though, it was about the future.

Raoul had always known unconditional love. He

didn't understand what it would be like for their daughter to question his feelings for her...didn't understand you could keep a child safe and warm and fed and still fail it completely.

Deciding she was too nervous to call, Julia grabbed her purse and bottle of water and headed for Raoul's office. She'd put it off all afternoon, now she had barely enough time to ask him and still make her doctor's appointment. His secretary, Debbie Elliott, looked up from her desk and smiled. "Hello, Ms. Parker. Please go right in."

"Isn't Mr. Oman busy?"

"Er...I have orders that you're always...." The woman lifted her shoulders.

With a wry shake of the head, Julia went into Raoul's office. His idea of "discreet" disagreed with her own, but she supposed he'd decided to trust his secretary.

"Julia," Raoul said, getting up. "Are you well?"

"Yes, of course." She stood for a moment, feeling awkward, then sighed. "I have an appointment with the obstetrician in a half hour. Would you like to go with me?"

He smiled. "I would love to join you."

"I'm...um, having another ultrasound."

"This is where we see a picture of the child—I mean, our daughter?"

Julia laughed. "Sort of a picture. It's made by sound waves, so it doesn't exactly compare to an Ansel Adams. Anyway, if you'd drive, I'll drink." She waved her quart bottle in the air and wrinkled her nose.

"Drink?"

"For some reason they still have me drinking lots of water before the test. Ultrasounds aren't painful, but when you're almost eight months pregnant and have to drink that much, it's darned uncomfortable. Mostly all I can think about is finding the nearest rest room."

Raoul chuckled. "Then I should definitely drive."

It was icy out, and as she drank her water, she marveled at the skill with which Raoul negotiated the slippery streets. She was tense driving on ice, and she'd lived in the midwest most of her life.

They reached the doctor's office and had the usual wait for the technician and equipment to be available. Julia had gone through several ultrasounds, and she'd learned to calculate the inevitable delays into the time allowed before she drank the required water. Otherwise, discomfort could turn into pure misery.

"And who is this with you?" asked the ultrasound technician, Carl Kirosaki. He looked surprised, probably because she'd made it clear there wasn't anyone who would come to be with her during her tests and checkups.

"Raoul Oman. I'm the father," Raoul said automatically. The two men shook hands, while Julia tried not to be annoyed that he'd announced their relationship, even though they hadn't discussed exactly *what* they should tell the doctor or his staff.

She got ready in an adjoining room and returned, more self-conscious than she'd been during all the other ultrasounds put together. It was silly. Raoul had seen more of her than any other man. For that matter, there wasn't a part of her that he *hadn't* seen, but now her stomach was big, and she'd never expected to see him again.

She was lying on the table and Carl was smearing the conducting gel on her abdomen when Dr. Svenson came in. Carl took care of the introductions, and she glimpsed relief in the doctor's face. He didn't care about alternative lifestyles and choice, but he said his patients did better when they had a strong family support structure.

Huh.

Raoul wasn't a support structure, he was a darned tsunami. Still, she had to admit the test went more easily with him holding her shoulders up and distracting her from the discomfort of needing a rest room.

"Is that her?" he asked, his breath lifting hair by Julia's ear.

Julia had more experience viewing the ultrasound, and her eyes softened at the grainy picture.

"Sure is," said Carl. "She's asleep at the moment, sucking her thumb." He pointed out the important features on the screen, always delighted to have an audience for the miracle of a new baby. He'd recently confided in Julia his plan to start medical school, specializing in obstetrics, of course.

Raoul stared at the image and tried to connect it with the child he'd felt kick in Julia's stomach. She was so small, and the first emotion to surface was protectiveness. The kind that came not from duty, but from inside his heart.

"How much does she need to gain to be all right?" he asked, riveted by the movement on the screen.

"I'm estimating her size at over four pounds," said Dr. Svenson. "At the current rate of gain, she should top five pounds before Julia's due date. I'll be happy with that."

Raoul eased his hand lower on Julia's back, hoping to make her more comfortable, though at the moment she was fixated on the video screen, watching the image. "Five pounds…that doesn't sound very big."

"Maybe not to a big guy like you, but it'll do. Well now, that does it." Dr. Svenson patted Julia's shoulder and handed the transducer to Carl Kirosaki. "Get dressed and we'll talk in my office."

She used the tissues he handed to her, wiping the gel from her abdomen while she hurried to the adjoining rest room.

"And that's the problem with my job," Carl complained to Raoul with a friendly smile. "Patients can't wait to leave me."

"You'll have to forgive her." Raoul smiled obligingly and accepted the videotape the technician took from the machine.

"It's the video of the baby," Carl explained. "I think she'll feel better about this one than the ones we've taken before."

Raoul held the tape and waited until a breathless Julia returned. Her cheeks were pink and she nervously tugged at her sweater. It was softer than the ones she'd worn to hide her pregnancy, and it molded gently over her tummy. Unsettled by emotions he couldn't quite process, he put an arm around her waist and pressed a hard, fast kiss on her mouth.

"Raoul?"

"You still need to see the doctor," he murmured.

It was difficult, being thrust into a new and unfamiliar world. All this time he'd fought the idea of marrying and having children, somehow thinking it would be boring and ordinary. But there was nothing ordinary about Julia, and nothing dull about seeing his daughter suck her thumb on a video monitor. He'd never realized a child in the womb did that.

In the office Dr. Svenson asked Julia questions and checked her blood pressure and pulse. He looked pleased and encouraged her to keep eating. "You're catching up now. I think everything will be fine."

"Thank you. You've been wonderful." Her face glowed and she couldn't stop smiling.

"You're doing all the hard work. I'll see you next week."

She practically floated out into the hallway. "Did you hear that? It's going to be all right."

Raoul smiled back. "I heard."

They stopped in the foyer of the professional building, Raoul frowning when he saw snow coming down beyond the glass doors. It was light but worrisome.

"Would it be acceptable if I took you directly home?" he asked, praying she'd say yes without a big argument. The thought of her driving back from the office made him crazy, but he'd known better than to insist. "I can bring your car over tomorrow. It'll be Saturday, so you won't need to go into work."

Julia cast him a sideways glance that told him she wasn't fooled for a moment. "All right, but I'll get the car myself, or take a taxi on Monday."

With an effort, he kept his mouth shut.

He wasn't the one who was pregnant, with a fraction of a man's strength. He honestly couldn't see why he shouldn't assist with small things like getting her car or providing food from his hotel's room-service kitchen.

Raoul drove carefully, slower than he normally would have. It wasn't entirely out of protectiveness, it was the lingering sense of peace he felt with Julia. Not that it would last. She and her prickly independence would find a reason to object to something soon enough. He even had a good idea what that "something'' might be, and knew he ought to discuss it with her.

"Do you want to come in?" Julia asked as he walked her to the door. She looked nervous again, so he shook his head.

"Here is my phone number at the hotel. Call if you need anything," Raoul said, pressing a card into her hand.

"You're still at the hotel?"

He looked into her upturned face. Snowflakes brushed her skin, clinging to her skin and hair. "I'm still deciding whether I should buy a house, as Kane suggested. It is easier to wait until I've made up my mind."

"I thought you didn't want a house."

"That was before I found out about this…." Raoul put his hand over her tummy, and she jerked slightly. "It changes things."

Her lashes drifted downward, but not before he saw regret in their depths.

"It's all right," he whispered. For the first time since learning of the baby, Raoul knew his anger was truly gone. It would have been different if Julia was different, but he couldn't stay upset with her.

"I didn't mean to hurt you."

"Perhaps this is our destiny. My grandfather would say our child is the result of fate, that we were predestined to reach this point from the moment we were born. And *Grand-mère*…she is a woman of faith. She would see God's hand in the little one's creation. They are wise people, I wouldn't want to dispute such a thing with them."

"I don't think resigning yourself to fate is any better than anger or cold duty," Julia murmured.

"I'm not resigned." Raoul brushed a kiss over her lips, chilled by the cold air and snow. "I'm intrigued."

Julia's eyes shot open. "Intrigued?"

"With the adventure. Go inside, *bien-aimée*. I will talk with you later."

He handed Julia the videotape from the ultrasound, then waited until the lock clicked behind her before walking to his car. He was still uncertain of what their future together might hold, but it no longer bothered him the way it had before. There were adjustments he had to make, and it wouldn't be easy, but it *was* intriguing.

The streets were white the next day, but the snow had stopped. Julia lit a fire in the kitchen fireplace and made herself pieces of wheat toast, dabbed with peanut butter, and smothered in sweet clover honey.

It was a treat she hadn't been able to enjoy during her entire pregnancy. Now she seemed able to eat anything, though not in large quantities. The baby was crowding her stomach to the point that she could only eat small meals throughout the day.

"Mmm." Julia licked honey from her fingers and reveled in the warmth of her early nineteenth-century brick fireplace. The house had been modernized and enlarged over the years, but there were still wonderful architectural features from its beginnings as a gatehouse, including oak beams across the ceilings and fireplaces in all the main rooms. It was one of the few structures from the original estate that had survived the Chicago fire in 1871.

She was contemplating a nap when someone rang the bell.

Raoul?

The possibility didn't bother her nearly as much as it would have a few weeks ago. Yawning, Julia walked into the living room and peeked through a window before answering. A delivery truck sat in the curving driveway that led up to the house.

"Yes?" she asked, cracking the door.

"Ms. Parker? I have some deliveries for you."

"I'm not expecting anything."

"Well, somebody sent it. We've got items from Toys 'n' Kids, Jackie's Baby Bunk…a bunch of places."

Her fingers tightened on the doorknob, her sleepy contentment evaporating.

Raoul.

"I didn't order anything, so you'll have to take it back."

"Ma'am, please. It's paid for, so why not take the stuff?"

"No. You just turn right around and tell them to refund Mr. Oman's money."

"But—"

"I said, no."

She shouldn't be angry with him; he was just the messenger—probably a college student earning extra bucks on the weekend. But she wasn't accepting anything more from Raoul, especially when they hadn't discussed it.

From the corner of her eye she saw a silver Mercedes drive up, then watched Raoul jump out and walk to the porch in an unhurried, confident stride.

"Is she being difficult?" he asked the young man and received a fervent nod. "Did you explain you would not get paid unless someone signed for the deliveries?"

"Didn't get a chance."

"*Raoul,*" Julia protested, furious he'd pull something so sneaky.

"She has a habit of doing that. Wait in the truck and I'll handle this."

Raoul turned to Julia, his eyes gleaming with laughter and something else...something that looked like a plea. When they were alone he opened the screen door and put his fingers across her lips.

"Yes, I should have asked," he said. "You are right. I made the initial arrangements before we talked the other day. But it would please me greatly if you would accept these small things for our daughter."

"Don't you see?" she whispered. "You're still manipulating me. You're asking, but you're also making it nearly impossible to refuse."

"He'll get paid," Raoul said quietly. "And I will give everything to a charity. No one will be hurt if you refuse."

No one but you, Julia wanted to scream.

Yet she could see he was trying. For the time being, maybe she should be content with the effort. They would have to compromise on a number of issues for the sake of the baby, and she was uncomfortably aware that she'd done little compromising herself.

"I...all right." It didn't come out as graciously as she would have liked, but like Raoul's effort, it was a start.

"Thank you, *chère.*" He leaned closer, and for a second she thought he would kiss her, but he didn't. "What room do you plan to use for a nursery?"

"I'll show you." Defeated, Julia turned and walked through the living room, Raoul close behind.

Her house was surprisingly large, something that

didn't show from the street. The additions to the original structure rambled in the back with odd passages and even odder-shaped rooms. She didn't use most of the extra space, but once the baby was big enough she planned to convert some of it into a play area. In the meantime, there was a room next to her own that would work well as a nursery.

"This is the one."

Raoul stood in the door, gazing around the freshly painted room. It was empty except for a plush carpet and an antique cedar chest along the back wall. Without a word he went to the chest and opened it. Inside were a few things—a stuffed animal, some clothing…a baby rattle—and a stab of sorrow went through him. He'd heard that women nested in the months of their pregnancy, gathering furniture and toys and clothing, but Julia had gotten practically nothing, fearing she'd lose the baby.

"I guess I should have gone shopping before now," she said. He looked up to see her rubbing her palms over her round stomach. "I just…"

"It's all right, I understand."

She nodded silently, and he sighed. He couldn't repair the past eight months, any more than he could heal her body from the condition that threatened her fertility. Instinctively, he'd always known that commitment meant sharing another's joys and sorrows. Especially the sorrows. It didn't speak well for him that he'd shied from that kind of responsibility.

"I should go out and help bring the load in," he said. He slipped past her, urgently needing physical activity. His feminine companions in the past had been uncomplicated—the only comfort they wanted was in bed. While he could offer Julia that same comfort, it wouldn't make anything better.

Unloading the delivery truck took numerous trips in and out, and Julia's eyes grew rounder and rounder as the stack grew. He'd gotten everything she'd looked or smiled at for longer than five seconds. And then some. She hadn't thought he'd paid that much attention, but she was wrong.

When she couldn't handle watching any longer, she hurried back to the kitchen. Milk and toast and honey, that's what she needed. Comfort food for her and the baby. After a while the opening and closing of the door stopped, and she heard the muffled sound of the truck starting.

"Do you have a knife and some other tools for me to use?" Raoul asked, coming into the kitchen. He'd removed his coat and his sleeves were rolled up, just like an ordinary guy getting ready to work around the house.

"A knife?"

"To open the boxes."

"I can do that. You don't have to bother."

His forehead crinkled in concentration. "It is no bother. And if you cannot climb stairs in your condition, you cannot assemble furniture. That is why you always take the elevator, is it not?"

Julia's mouth opened, then shut again quickly. Raoul was far too observant for comfort.

"That looks good. May I have some?"

Without waiting for an answer, he lifted her hand holding a piece of toast. In two bites it was gone.

"Mmm, I love honey," Raoul murmured, sucking each of her fingers into his mouth in turn, his tongue caressing the sensitive space between them. By the time he was done, they were both breathing quickly.

"That isn't...maybe I should make some coffee," she said. "Or tea. Or something."

"There's no hurry. It will take some time to finish in the nursery. Where is your toolbox?" he asked, his voice harsh.

She pulled her hand free and waved to a cupboard near the back door. "In there."

His face was rigid with restraint, and he left after finding the tools he needed. Julia wrapped her arms around the swell of her tummy and tried to regain her equilibrium.

Raoul knew he could seduce her; she hadn't exactly been standoffish, even after his arrival in Chicago. And she couldn't blame him for making sex the common point between them. Love wasn't part of the equation—physical attraction was the only constant.

It was getting late when Julia stirred from her sleepy melancholy. She didn't have any Arabian coffee, but she knew to make it strong. *Really* strong. At their hotel in Washington she'd taken a swallow from his cup one morning and nearly gagged.

"How is it going?" she asked, standing at the door of the nursery, mug in hand.

Raoul looked up and smiled slowly. In Hasan a palace servant would have taken care of such tasks, and he could have paid someone to put everything together here in America. But it wouldn't have proven anything to Julia, or to himself. And there was a certain satisfaction in doing things with your own hands.

"It's going," he said. "But now I understand what a friend of mine calls the ABC nightmare."

"What's that?"

"The instruction to fit slot A into slot B when there isn't a slot B. I am told the words guaranteed to strike terror into a parent's heart are *some assembly required.*"

Julia laughed, and he was glad to see her expression relax. He shouldn't have gotten close in the kitchen, but his body didn't always cooperate with good sense.

"Maybe some coffee will help," she said, holding out a cup.

"*Mon tresór,* you read my mind." He took a long swallow, nodding his approval. "Excellent. I fear most of the coffee in America is somewhat like dishwater."

"Not everyone likes to go into caffeine overdrive," Julia teased. "Some of us even like herbal tea."

"Worse than dishwater," he pronounced.

"Well, I'm stuck with herbal tea for the time being."

She'd put her hand on her stomach again, and drifted around the room, touching the various items he'd unpacked. He watched carefully. If there was anything she didn't like he would find something else.

He'd already attached the mobile she'd admired above the crib and she touched the dancing feline figures with a soft smile. Her black-and-white cat·was curled in the middle of the new mattress, apparently convinced the new furniture and toys were entirely for his benefit.

"Hey, Muppet," she said, lifting him in her arms. "Are you being a problem?"

"He has been wary," Raoul said, setting his empty cup aside. There was no questioning Muppet's gender—he showed an unmistakable jealousy of another masculine presence. But they had reached an understanding that stopped short of bloodshed…barely.

The cat reclined on his back with an indecently pleased expression, one paw on Julia's breast, his tail switching smugly.

"You got an awful lot of things for the baby," she said.

"Not so much." Raoul set the changing table he'd just assembled against the wall. The few items he'd purchased seemed inadequate, but he would continue looking for items to please her. There were so many antiques in her house, he knew she might enjoy something older, with more history.

She had excellent taste, but then everything about Julia Parker was elegant; he'd appreciated that quality in her from the beginning.

"Shall I fix some dinner?" she asked while he gathered the last of the boxes together.

It was tempting to stay, but he didn't have a great deal of restraint at the moment. "Thank you, but I have a prior engagement. I should go."

"Oh. Sorry. I didn't mean to keep you from your plans," she stuttered.

Was that a flash of jealousy in her gold eyes? Raoul hadn't intended to make her question him, but it was interesting to think she might feel that way.

"You didn't keep me, I wanted to stay. I will see you on Monday," he said. "Call the hotel if there is something you need."

"Yes, of course. And Raoul, thank you for this…" She motioned around the room, her face soft with emotion. "It feels closer now. Like it's really going to happen."

"It is, *chère*. You will see, everything will be all right."

"Prior engagement?" Julia murmured as the sound of Raoul's Mercedes faded. "What do you think that means, Muppet?"

Muppet yawned.

She put him down and looked around the nursery. Thanks to Raoul it was now a nursery, not an empty room. She hadn't even realized how much it bothered her to have nothing for the baby. It had almost been superstitious, as if buying things might jinx an already precarious situation.

It was strange, but Raoul's reassurances *did* make her feel better. Maybe it was because she didn't feel alone any longer, which was strange as well. Raoul hadn't wanted a family, but he was trying to help her, to make her feel safe and secure. How many men would do that? How many men would put aside their own feelings and emotionally support the mother of their unwanted child?

Julia worked for a long time, sorting Raoul's gifts and putting them away. When she was done the nursery looked like every woman's dream—cozy and warm, a sweet little nest for a baby girl.

"What do you think, Muppet?"

Muppet "marrowed" at the crib, now occupied by a myriad stuffed animals, and flicked his tail in displeasure.

Smiling tiredly, Julia sat in the new rocking chair and closed her eyes. It still worried her, the idea of letting Raoul be part of their lives, though not as much as before. Raoul was a good man—good in a way she'd never known. He might be too controlling, but that was only a part of him.

The doorbell broke into her reflections, and a flash of elation went through her. It had to be Raoul coming back. She mentally reviewed the contents of her refrigerator as she hurried to the front door, deciding what she could put together for a late meal.

"Julia, sorry to barge in, but we've been chased out of my house," exclaimed Sharon Waterton. Behind her were Lauren and Maggie. "Can we come in? We brought pizza." She gestured with a large flat box.

"Oh…sure."

Of the three women, Lauren looked the most uncomfortable, and she shot Julia an apologetic glance. "We weren't actually chased out," she explained. "But Jack was working and it got a little noisy. Then Maggie said your house was close by, and she didn't think you'd mind if we came over."

"You know men and their tools," Sharon said cheerfully.

Actually, Julia didn't have a clue about men and tools. Her father hadn't been the "handy" type, nor had either of the men in her two disastrous past relationships. But she was glad for the distraction—she hadn't socialized since getting pregnant and hadn't realized how much she'd missed the company.

They ate in the kitchen, with everyone complimenting her on the old fireplace and the way she'd decorated with copper pots and herbs.

"I don't think Lauren and Sharon have ever been here. Why don't you show them around?" Maggie suggested as they washed the few dishes they'd used.

Julia looked at her friend with a moderate amount of suspicion. She'd gotten wind of a "surprise" baby

shower being planned at work…with her being the
guest of honor. It was a tradition at Kane Haley, Inc.—
she'd helped throw a few herself. But if this was the
planning committee's not-so-subtle way of finding out
what she needed, she had a surprise for *them.* After
Raoul's shopping spree, she was supplied for a dozen
babies.

"Sure," Julia said, deciding to play along. She was
proud of her house, so it wasn't a hardship showing it
off.

"How beautiful," Lauren exclaimed when they
reached the nursery. "It must have taken months to do
this."

Julia couldn't help it, she laughed. That morning the
room had been practically empty, now it was practically perfect. All she'd done was look and admire, and
Raoul had taken care of the rest. Maybe this was a
good time to let them know he was the baby's father.
Of course, she knew that Maggie suspected, but Maggie was the most discreet person in the world.

"Actually," Julia said, "this is all from Raoul. He
was here earlier."

Lauren and Sharon spun in unison.

"Sheik Oman?" Lauren squeaked. "Are you serious? He must be smitten big-time."

Smitten.

Right.

Julia let out a breath. "Well, actually, Raoul is
the…uh, father. Of my baby."

They stared at her for so long she wondered if they
were all right. Maybe it was too big a shock, realizing
she'd gotten herself pregnant with a man like Raoul.
He *was* exceptionally attractive. He'd made most of the
women at Kane Haley, Inc., sigh with undisguised lust;

the ones who weren't sighing were either married or dead.

"We met at that June conference in Washington, D.C., but he didn't know I was pregnant until he got to Chicago," Julia added hastily. She was beginning to understand the depths of Raoul's pride, and couldn't let them think he'd just ignored her for seven months. "He wants to get married, but I'm still thinking about it."

"You're not sure if you want to marry *Raoul Oman?*" Mouth still open in shock, Lauren staggered back to sit on the cedar chest, but she missed it and landed hard on the floor.

"Are you all right?" Julia asked, alarmed.

Lauren climbed to her feet again and rubbed her bruised bottom. "I'm just fine. But I have serious questions about you!"

Chapter Eight

I'm just fine. But I have serious questions about you!

All the next day, the memory of Lauren's stunned face kept making Julia laugh. She hadn't intended to reveal Raoul's proposal, but she'd been so anxious they know he was being honorable that she'd let it slip.

A man's honor wasn't as simple as she'd always thought. It mattered to Raoul in a deep, immeasurable way that he do the right thing. He wanted to be respected, but it was *doing* right that counted most to him. She was still mulling it over on Monday morning as she paid the taxi driver and walked into the building. Raoul had called and offered to pick her up, but she'd said no, it didn't make sense since his hotel was in the opposite direction.

In her office Julia sank into her chair and automatically glanced at the refrigerator, wondering what Raoul had put in it for her today. She was getting spoiled, but she'd never been spoiled before and couldn't help enjoying the experience.

Sharon Waterton came in and plopped down on a chair. "I'm hungry. What did you bring?"

Julia grinned. She'd been sharing the food, since it was always more than she could eat by herself, and Raoul would just throw it out when he brought the next load—which he did on a daily basis. She opened the refrigerator and saw a Greek salad with olives and feta cheese. Behind that were a couple of fat turkey-and-Swiss-cheese sandwiches and the usual milk, prepared fruit and pudding.

"Greek salad or turkey sandwich?" she asked.

"No contest. Sandwich."

"Okay." Julia handed one over. "But you should know, Raoul is the one bringing the goodies."

Sharon choked on a bite of her sandwich. "And you don't want to marry him? The man feeds you, is yummier than New York cheesecake, and has the nicest behind—next to my husband's—that I've ever seen on a man."

"No comment."

The baby began kicking and Julia put her hand over the squirming infant with a contented smile. It was starting to feel as if an entire soccer team was practicing inside her stomach.

The phone rang and Sharon got up, waving goodbye with a mouthed "Thank you."

"Julia Parker speaking," Julia said into the receiver.

"Hello, Ms. Parker, this is the Seaton Birth Learning Center. Just wanted you to know we've been able to schedule your first Lamaze class for tonight. Do you want us to notify Mr. Oman, as well?"

Julia had been doodling on her calendar, but now she froze. "Mr. Oman?"

"Er...yes. He's your Lamaze coach, isn't he?"

Instantly, red rose before her eyes. She was angry, but she was also disappointed. "We'll be in touch," she snapped and slammed the phone down.

Damn him.

She charged out, heading straight for Raoul's office. "Is he in?" she growled to his secretary. "Is he alone?"

Debbie Elliott's welcoming smile turned cautious. "Yes."

"Good." Julia threw the door open and stormed inside. "How could you do it?" she demanded. "You said you weren't trying to control me, and you then do something like this behind my back. I really believed you were making an effort."

He calmly put down his pen, got up and closed the door. "Do what behind your back?"

"The Seaton Birth Learning Center just called. It seems 'our' initial Lamaze class has been scheduled for tonight. You came to my house on Saturday and said all those things, but they didn't mean anything, did they?"

Raoul uttered a silent curse. "Julia, I didn't do that."

"No? Then how did the class get scheduled?"

She was furious, and rightfully so. He'd have suggested she sit down, but knew it would only make things worse. "Yes, I did ask we be scheduled for classes, but that was over two weeks ago. I called last Friday and told them to wait because I needed to talk to you about it first."

"Someone obviously didn't get the message."

"And I will talk to them about the error. But you cannot blame me for wanting to attend these classes and to be present for the birth of our child."

Julia let out a long, shuddering breath and sank onto

the couch. "This isn't going to work," she muttered. "I was crazy ever to think it could."

"I didn't know you had ever thought it possible."

She tapped her fingers on the arm of the couch, beautiful and flushed and so miserable he cursed to himself again. It was a hard thing for a man to realize he was the kind of man his woman *didn't* want. And even harder to change—but he was trying. With every breath in his body he was trying.

"Julia," Raoul said, sitting next to her and taking her hand. She didn't resist, but he could tell she was unwilling to share even that small contact. "I want the best for you. Perhaps my actions are misplaced, but I intend well."

She stirred restlessly. "You don't trust me to take care of myself or the baby. That's the real problem. You think you have to take care of everything and make all the decisions because I'm incapable of doing it myself."

His eyes widened, horrified she would think something so impossible. "That isn't true. You are intelligent and accomplished. You worked yourself through school and succeeded at great odds. I can imagine no finer mother for a child."

She looked at him unhappily. "We're just too different. Don't you see, Raoul? You're a member of the royal family in Hasan—Sheik Raoul Oman, accustomed to issuing orders and having them obeyed without question. While I'm just an ordinary American woman who works for a living."

"There is nothing ordinary about you, Julia. Trust me, an *ordinary* woman could not have tempted me so much I failed to use protection."

"That's just about sex."

"It is about a woman who fascinates me. One who is stubborn and independent and won't let me be part of her life," he growled. "You have never taken an order from me in the entire time we've known each other."

"Except in bed," she shot back. "You wouldn't have it any other way."

"*Mon Dieu.*" Raoul threw up his hands. "You still have not figured it out, have you, Julia? You were in control, not me. I would have done anything to please you, and I would cut off my arm now rather than cause you pain. But you seem to have forgotten I cannot just walk out of your life."

She didn't believe him. The tawny gold of her eyes was too wary, too hurt from the past unkindnesses of men unworthy to be members of his gender. For an instant Raoul fought panic, a sense of something greater than himself slipping away before he had a chance to understand it.

"*Chère,* please. You are right to be cautious. In truth, you have no reason to trust me, but I swear I am trying. I planned to show you the class brochures this morning—only because I hoped you would want me to attend with you."

Julia dropped her gaze to the hand Raoul still held. She'd given up the idea of natural childbirth out of the fear she'd lose the baby…and because she was alone. She could have asked one of her friends to be her Lamaze coach, but they were busy with their lives and she hated to impose. She'd never even considered talking to Raoul. Maybe she was wrong to be upset. Raoul had been forced into the position of being a father, yet he wanted to be with her when the baby was born…a prospect that seemed to make a lot of men uncomfortable.

"Maybe I overreacted," she said slowly.

"You were right to be angry."

"May I see the brochures?"

"Of course." Raoul released her hand and went to his desk. He handed her a sheaf of papers and she glanced through them. The literature extolled the virtues of Lamaze and discussed various myths about childbirth. It was the same place that Sharon and Jack had discussed using for their Lamaze classes.

"Why did you schedule the first class two weeks into the future?" she murmured.

"The center has a waiting list. They said they would notify me if they had an opening."

Julia sneaked a peek at him. She was almost certain he hadn't mentioned the waiting list just to push her into attending this class. The Seaton Birth Learning Center was popular and well-thought of; it might easily have a waiting list. Although it had a birthing facility as well as offering classes, Dr. Svenson had recommended the birth take place at the hospital because of her medical history.

"You do not have to attend the class, Julia. Or you can have someone else coach you for the birth."

She sighed, knowing what it had cost Raoul to make that offer. "I guess we could go to the first class, and see how it goes."

"Really? You would be willing?" The eagerness in his face made him look young and boyish and more handsome than ever.

"You're aware they show films about childbirth," Julia felt obliged to say. "Real birth scenes, with fainting fathers and women sweaty and red in the face from contractions.''

"You are trying to scare me off?"

"I'm sure it alarms most men."

"I am not most men. It disturbs me to know the discomfort you face in childbirth," he said thoughtfully, "but I must know how to make it easier for you. Would you like to have dinner, and go to the class afterward?"

Julia shook her head. Much as she disliked admitting it, even to herself, she'd gotten to the point where she didn't have enough energy to work eight or nine hours.

"I...um, talked to the head of my department last week about working shorter days until after the baby comes, so I'll be going home early—around two. We discussed the possibility of my working part-time at the house, but the company doesn't have a policy on that yet."

"I will speak to Kane."

She rolled her eyes. "He's not going to change company policy because of me, Raoul."

"I can be very persuasive."

Didn't she know it!

"Well, if you can get Kane to agree, it would be great. Work-at-home programs make good sense with so much technology available," Julia said, deciding not to make an issue of Raoul's "persuasiveness."

A smile twinkled in Raoul's eyes, but it faded with the sound of excited voices outside his office. He looked at her frantically. "Please, Julia, do not get upset. I believe my parents have just arrived."

Her heart sank to the general vicinity of her ankles. "Your...parents?"

"From Hasan. I called a few days ago and spoke to

my sister about the baby coming. She was to tell the family, but to keep them home. I should have realized their silence meant they were on their way to the United States."

Julia gulped.

She was a true American, democratic to her bones, but it was intimidating to think of meeting the future king of another country—especially when she was carrying that future king's first grandchild. "Are you serious?"

"Entirely."

The door burst open and a beautiful woman in a dove-gray suit swept inside, followed by a man who looked like an older version of Raoul. Like Raoul, he was handsome beyond reason. But they both stopped dead in their tracks under their son's intimidating scowl.

The woman spoke first, her hand fluttering to the pearls around her neck. "It is wonderful to see you, my son."

"Wonderful? I asked you to stay in Hasan."

"We…er…are just here briefly. Your father wanted to deliver some papers for you to sign."

"Papers? You could not send a courier for this?" Raoul demanded.

"Not after hearing such glad news about a grandchild." Her gaze flashed to Julia and a shrewd smile curved her lips. "Is this your Julia? The one who will not marry you?"

If anything, Raoul's face turned grimmer. "Don't start, Mother. We will make our own decisions. Julia, these are my parents, Rihanna and Jamal Oman."

Julia inched her way to the edge of the couch and he turned automatically to help her. She couldn't rise gracefully with a stomach the size of a small beach ball, so the best she hoped to manage was not to fall on her face in front of the royal couple.

She and Rihanna Oman locked gazes for a long minute, then the older woman smiled again—a warm, loving, welcoming smile that didn't judge or condemn.

"What a lovely child you are," Rihanna said warmly. "Has my son given you a difficult time? He is excellent at that."

Julia didn't know what to say, because she'd either make things worse for Raoul or embarrass him, but he protested with another loud exclamation.

"Hush, son."

Rihanna pulled Julia into a close embrace. She wore an exotic perfume and was obviously rich and pampered, but for the first time in longer than she could remember, Julia knew she was being hugged by a real mother.

"We only wished to meet you, little one," Rihanna said after releasing her. She put out her hand, then hesitated. "May I?"

Julia nodded and Raoul's mother placed her fingers over the bulge of her stomach. Tears filled the older woman's eyes as the baby kicked.

"It's a girl," Julia whispered, afraid she'd see disappointment in the Omans' faces. Her ideas about the Middle East were more muddled than ever, but she was still afraid that daughters weren't valued as much as sons.

"Daughters are the dearest of treasures," Rihanna said eagerly. "We were twice blessed."

"Our daughter, Fatima, is a gifted doctor," Jamal Oman said, speaking for the first time. His expression was reserved, but Julia had a feeling he was a kind man. "And Jasmine has brought great honor to Hasan through her art."

"Yes, Julia knows all of this. Where are the papers you wish me to sign?" Raoul asked impatiently. If he'd known his parents would show up in Chicago, he would have warned her. Hell, he would have gotten her out of the city. Heaven alone knew what she was thinking. What if she believed he'd encouraged them to come to manipulate or force her into marriage?

He would lose all hope of getting close to her.

"I'd better go," Julia said. She smiled at his parents. "It was nice meeting you. My due date is in March, if you'd like...." she shrugged diffidently.

"Thank you." His mother dabbed at her eyes with a handkerchief. "We are so grateful you will let us visit our grandchild. You must now consider yourself part of our family."

"Thank you." With a last, swift glance in his direction, Julia hurried away. He couldn't tell what she was thinking, and after the earlier fiasco of the Lamaze classes he was afraid it couldn't be good.

"How could you, Mother?" he asked when they were alone. "Julia is a strong woman, you cannot push her."

"I didn't push, son." Rihanna looked him square in the eye with the same expression that used to mean handing over his car keys. "But if you let that sweet child out of your life, you will regret it always. When two people are made for each other, it is a gift from heaven. Now, discuss business with your father, then we will leave."

"You're leaving today?"

"Yes." She gave him a small, satisfied smile. "We are going to this Disneyland park in California. Your father wishes to ride the Pirates of the Caribbean."

"You're kidding." Raoul shook his head, uncertain if this was one of her jokes.

Jamal Oman chuckled. "Not at all, son. We are going to have an American grandchild. I wish to be familiar with the many ways we can spoil her."

Before Julia left for the day, a small package was delivered to her office. She opened it and found the double strand of pink pearls that she'd seen Rihanna Oman wearing. They were undoubtedly real, with a tasteful diamond-and-gold clasp. The card read:

For the charming mother of my grandchild and newest member of our family.

                                        Rihanna.

Julia gulped, and the pearls slid from her fingers to the desk. She wasn't an expert on jewelry, but she knew this wasn't an average, run-of-the-mill strand of pearls—they were the most beautiful things she'd ever seen. She couldn't accept such a valuable gift; she'd have to return them to Raoul tonight and ask him to smooth things over with his family.

He'd called to set a time to pick her up to attend the class, apologizing again for his parents' unexpected arrival. She'd laughed it off, mostly because she'd seen his chagrin when they walked into the office.

Grinning at the memory, Julia put the pearls in her purse. On her way out she met Kane Haley at the elevator, coat over one arm, and gave him a strained smile. It was uncomfortable talking to him after what had happened several weeks before. And she still didn't know exactly why it had been so important for him to know about her being pregnant.

"Hi, Kane."

"Julia." He glanced down at her stomach with a peculiar look on his face. "I guess you really are that far along."

"Is that a polite way of saying I'm getting big?"

"I…no. That is…*damn.* I'm so sorry," he said, an endearingly sheepish expression on his face. "Have you and Raoul worked anything out?"

Kane Haley might be the president of the company, but she wasn't letting him off that easily. "Worked out what?"

"About…" He gestured toward her tummy.

She lifted her eyebrow in an imitation of Raoul's haughty style of inquiry—the one that said *someone* was being awfully impertinent. The elevator doors opened and Julia stepped inside, Kane close behind her.

"Julia?"

"I think that's between us, don't you?"

"Uh, yeah. Sure. Sorry."

Hiding a smile, Julia pushed the button for the ground floor, while he chose the fourteenth. She wasn't that upset with Kane. Raoul had learned about her pregnancy in less than ideal circumstances, but nothing could have kept him from realizing he was the father. She'd been foolish to think it was possible.

Kane hesitated before getting out. "Raoul and I have been friends for over ten years, but I would never have said anything if I'd known he was there."

She lifted her shoulders in a small shrug. "Forget it, Kane. He would have found out sooner or later."

"Well, if there's anything you need…let me know."

Kane left hastily, and Julia wondered if they'd ever

have a comfortable conversation again. Not that she knew the president that well, but he was the boss, and she'd rather get along with him. Besides, she was grateful for his support of the day-care center. The construction was on schedule, so with any luck it would be open soon after she returned from maternity leave.

She made a mental note to tell Sharon she couldn't attend the next committee meeting on the center because of her changed work schedule, and hurried to her car. On the hood was a single, flame-red rose. She didn't need a note to know who had left it there.

Julia inhaled the blossom's perfume, knowing she had a ridiculous smile on her face.

"Just relax," said the Lamaze instructor. She was a buxom redhead with a tiny waist and an excess of perky energy. "What we've all forgotten is that a woman's body knows how to give birth. It's a beautiful and natural thing."

They were sitting on the floor and Julia leaned against Raoul to ease the strain on her back. She was surrounded by earth mothers—women who had known to bring pillows to sit on, who were round and comfortable and at ease with the whole process of being coached and giving birth.

They'd listened to a short lecture, and were now going to practice concentration and breathing techniques. This was the accelerated class, one for women and coaches who had either already had other babies, or who were too close to their delivery date to go through a longer series of classes. Julia didn't fall into either category, though her due date was closer than she liked to think about.

She shifted on her borrowed pillow and Raoul's fingers massaged the aching center of her discomfort. He didn't say anything, and she could tell he was intent on the lessons they were supposed to be learning.

An unpleasant niggle of emotion went through Julia as she remembered the Lamaze instructor's enthusiastic greeting for Raoul and his focused gaze on her. Yet, how could she blame him? Compared to her, Patty was cute, slim and seemed to be in a perpetual good mood. Was Patty the reason he hadn't stayed at her house for dinner on Saturday night?

"Are you all right?" Raoul whispered when Julia squirmed again.

"Fine. I'm just not used to sitting on the floor." He shifted so she rested between his outstretched legs and could lean more fully on his chest. It felt so nice she closed her eyes and concentrated on the steady beating of his heart.

"Are you ready?" Raoul asked when Patty had finally finished talking, and they were supposed to practice breathing exercises.

Julia reluctantly opened her eyes. "I guess."

He'd listened far more attentively than she, so she followed his lead, breathing and counting when he said to, and focusing on the slow strokes of his hands over her abdomen. It shouldn't have been sensual, but it seemed erotic in a sweet, safe way.

"That's excellent," Patty said, interrupting as she knelt by them. "You're in perfect harmony. Have you done this before?"

"No. Trust me, I'd remember having a baby," Julia replied dryly.

Patty chuckled in perfect good humor. "Of course. You're doing great, keep it up." She went on to the next couple, encouraging them in the same bouncy cheerleader style.

There wasn't a single reason the other woman should be so annoying, except for the little problem Julia was having with jealousy. She wiggled, putting her hands on Raoul's thighs to pull herself farther upright.

"Ah, *chère*. Don't get up just yet. You will make me embarrass myself," Raoul muttered.

He was breathing more quickly, and she frowned. What was he talking about? An instant later, she recognized an insistent pressure against her bottom—evidence of a very aroused male.

It had better be for me, she thought irritably.

Which was hardly fair. She'd refused to marry him, couldn't have sex even if she was willing because of a high-risk pregnancy, and had tricked him into getting her that way in the first place. But still, it had better be for her.

"That's all, folks," Patty announced a little while later. "Be sure to practice your exercises and read the material you were given. I'll see you next week."

Julia was silent on the walk out to Raoul's Mercedes. She was getting so mixed up about him, her heart and her head telling her different things. And now that she'd met his parents it was even harder to think straight.

"I just wish you'd take those pearls back," she muttered, returning to the discussion they'd had earlier. "They're too valuable."

"My mother wishes you to have them."

"You don't give a complete stranger costly jewelry."

"You are not a stranger, you are the mother of her grandchild. This means much in my culture."

She let out an exasperated breath, knowing the necklace wasn't really the problem. If she let Raoul be her Lamaze coach, they would be practicing together, alone in her house. Physical contact was part of the package and she was far too vulnerable.

"Raoul...I really can't make love, not with the baby," she said impulsively, then groaned. Her mouth was a loose cannon these days.

He froze in the act of taking his keys from his pocket. "Is this about my lack of control earlier?"

"No...I mean...I don't know what I mean."

"I want you, Julia, but I know it isn't good for the baby. You don't have to worry about being alone with me."

It wasn't Raoul she was worried about, only she didn't want to say so. "Was it *me* who aroused you, or perky Patty?" she asked, hating herself for wanting to know.

"The instructor? What are you talking about?"

"She's very attractive."

"She is?"

Julia practically giggled at the perplexed look on Raoul's face and a bubble of pleasure filled her. He hadn't noticed Patty's high, generous breasts or skinny waist. She wanted to clap her hands and do a little dance, even knowing it was stupid and selfish to want his full attention.

She ought to have trusted him. Raoul might not love her, but he'd made his own kind of commitment to their strange relationship. He wouldn't betray her.

"Sorry," Julia whispered, putting her arms around his neck and snuggling as close as her tummy would allow. "I think my hormones have gone south."

A smile played on Raoul's mouth, and he cupped her face with both hands. "How far south?"

"Clear to my feet," she said quickly, knowing exactly what part of her anatomy he hoped her hormones had fled to. "You must have seen how swollen my ankles are."

He kissed her, a single chaste kiss with closed lips. "Your ankles are beautiful, as are you. Now let me take you home to your nice warm fireplace and suspicious cat."

"Don't mind Muppet. He's just jealous."

"Does he have reason to be?"

Julia smiled noncommittally. She couldn't answer such a loaded question. Though it really wasn't the question that was loaded...it was the answer.

Chapter Nine

"**S**urprise!"

Julia clapped a hand over her heart and laughed. She was actually surprised, too, though she'd suspected a baby shower was in the offing. She just hadn't expected it today.

The employees' lunchroom was festooned with pink-and-white streamers, along with flowers and baby rattles. It seemed as if everyone who worked at Kane Haley, Inc., was there—male *and* female—along with Jennifer Holder who was still on maternity leave.

"I couldn't miss your party," Jennifer declared, giving her a hug. "You and the others gave me such a beautiful shower before Jason was born."

"When are you coming back to work?"

"Pretty soon. But it's hard." Jennifer rocked the baby in her arms, a diaper thrown over one shoulder. "I hate the thought of leaving him. It'll be better when the day-care center opens."

Julia nodded. She hadn't even given birth and she was already suffering from separation anxiety.

Across the room Raoul lifted a cup of punch in a silent toast, smiling at her. He hadn't repeated his request she tell everyone he was the baby's father, though people probably suspected. The only ones who knew for certain were Sharon, Maggie and Lauren, and they wouldn't have said anything. Julia made up her mind to find a way of making a formal announcement during the party.

He deserved that much.

To be honest, he deserved more than that, but she wasn't any closer to deciding what to do about it.

Was it really possible for a man who'd avoided marriage and children like the plague to evolve into a good husband and father? Not that she intended to marry him, Julia assured herself quickly. But he was obviously going to be a part of their daughter's life.

"This is a happy moment, *chère,*" Raoul murmured as he walked up. "Smile for your friends."

She smiled, a warm sensation curling around her heart. She had a lot of friends, though she'd done a good job of keeping them at a distance, particularly during her pregnancy.

"Are we still meeting tonight at your house to practice?" he asked quietly.

"Sure, but you just want to get your hands on my body," she replied.

Raoul cast a startled glance at Julia. Her voice had sounded light and flirtatious. "Your body is worth touching," he breathed into her ear, a moment before Maggie and Lauren swept her away.

He stood shoulder to shoulder with Kane, Rafe Mitchell and another man who had been introduced as

Jack Waterton. Jack, he understood, was married to the curvaceous Sharon, who was expecting a baby a couple of months after Julia. The women pursued some sort of name competition and he watched, his forehead crinkled in perplexity.

"Games are a tradition at baby showers," Jack muttered. "Sharon's already had one, and you wouldn't believe the stuff they think is fun. It'll be your turn next, Rafe. Wait till Lauren gets pregnant, and you have to pretend the whole thing is cute and interesting."

As Rafe shuddered, Raoul wondered what Kane was thinking. Kane had confided his reasons for questioning Julia about her pregnancy, and from the grimly intense look on his friend's face, he suspected Kane was again evaluating the mother-potential of the assembled women.

Somehow, Raoul preferred his own predicament.

Kane's unknown child had been conceived in a doctor's office, without his knowledge or presence. *His* child had been conceived of passion—without his consent, but he'd participated fully in the act, enjoying every moment.

Julia's hair was soft around her face, her eyes bright with laughter as she played the little games the others had devised. Cake and ice cream was served and eaten, along with various other treats appropriate for an expectant mother.

When the time came for opening the small mountain of gifts, Julia paused, her gaze seeking him out. She cleared her throat and the chatter died down, everyone waiting for her to speak.

"As many of you may have guessed, I knew Raoul Oman before he came to work at Kane Haley."

Raoul straightened, praying he knew what she was going to announce.

She cleared her throat again. ''And I think he should help unwrap all these presents, because he's the baby's father…and he cares about her very much.''

A loud exclamation went up, with a round of congratulations and slaps on his back. A surge of excited women pulled Raoul from his location with the men, and into a chair next to Julia, where he squeezed her hand in a silent thank-you.

It couldn't have been easy, telling everyone. She had a stubborn, stiff-necked pride that dared the world to say she was incapable of tackling life on her own. He was only just beginning really to understand how important it was for Julia to feel she had control.

As the wrapping paper mounted and the gifts emerged, Raoul smiled and admired and could barely keep his eyes off her. She'd blossomed in the past weeks. He'd heard his married friends speak of a woman's radiance when she was carrying a baby, but he'd never believed it until now.

Julia was incandescent.

Because of their shopping trip together, he was familiar with baby things, and he could tell her friends and co-workers had chosen carefully. A group had gone together on a year's worth of diaper service, there were books on child-rearing, toys and clothing, along with personal gifts for Julia. But when she uncovered a hand-carved walnut cradle from Jack and Sharon Waterton, she nearly cried.

''It's beautiful,'' she gasped.

''I know you've got a crib already,'' Sharon said. ''But I was glad to see Raoul hadn't gotten a cradle with all the other stuff.'' She looked at Raoul and wrinkled her nose. "You sure didn't leave much for us to get the baby, you know."

He smiled, realizing Julia had ensured her closest friends knew he was doing his duty by her. "I did not intend to make it difficult, only to provide for our child."

"That's all right. Julia deserves the best."

Raoul agreed with the casual comment, knowing the line between duty and his heart had disappeared. It was as if his soul was unfolding, discovering new depths and feelings he'd never known existed. And Julia was the core of everything, seeming closer and more necessary than the air he breathed.

In the background a baby began crying and he could see the mother trying to soothe the unhappy infant. Matthew Holder, Kane Haley, Inc.'s Director of Human Resources, took the child and turned toward Raoul with a wicked smile.

"I think the new daddy should get a taste of what's coming," he said over the screams.

"Matt, don't you dare!" exclaimed Jennifer.

"I'm told Raoul does everything well, let's see how he handles this."

In short order the squalling infant was deposited in Raoul's arms, and he looked down, half in alarm, half in fascination. It was so tiny, with hands and arms that flailed in the air, and a small red face that voiced its displeasure with the world.

Out of an instinct he didn't know he possessed, he patted the child's back and spoke softly in French. And, whether it was because of the unfamiliar language or being held by a stranger, the infant stopped crying and looked at him with wide, wondering eyes.

"Ohmigod, he's got the touch," someone declared.

The men present groaned, saying he was ruining things for the rest of them, while the woman crowed with delight and told Julia how lucky she was. Pleased he'd been successful, Raoul gazed back at the baby. *This* was what he'd avoided all his life? Dreaded? How could you dread something so tiny and precious?

"How large is he?" Raoul asked Jennifer.

"At our last checkup, Jason weighed over eleven pounds."

"Eleven pounds?" Startled, Raoul looked at Julia's small stomach, panic crowding his throat as he remembered the doctor explaining the weight of the baby she carried. Jason was more than twice the size of his daughter and yet seemed so tiny and breakable he was almost afraid to touch him.

"Jason's a little slugger," Matt said, scooping the baby from Raoul's arms and cradling him against his shoulder. "He's going to be the next quarterback for the Chicago Bulls—they want him in the lineup next week."

"Stop it, Matt," Jennifer scolded.

"Just kidding, sweetheart." He blew her a kiss that was full of love.

Raoul glanced at Julia, finally understanding the depth of the fear she'd felt for so many months. It awed him, what she'd gone through. Reaching out, he put his hand over the swell of Julia's stomach. A determined little foot thudded against his palm, and he smiled with relief. Small, yes, but strong like her mother.

"Raoul?" Julia looked worried, because he'd rarely touched her stomach without permission.

"It is all right, *bien-aimée*. I wished to reassure myself."

"About what?"

"That she is well."

The last gift was handed to Julia and she took it, her gaze still locked with his.

"Go on," he murmured.

Julia dragged her attention to the large, professionally wrapped present on her lap. She checked the tag, somehow not surprised to see it was from Raoul. She unwrapped it slowly, wondering what he could possibly have bought after having had an entire truckload of things delivered to her house.

Inside the box she pushed aside pink tissue paper and held her breath. It was an antique patchwork quilt, one she'd admired a few days before. She lifted it out to find the matching baby quilt beneath.

"This is the one..." She swallowed and tried to keep from crying. "The one in the antique store."

"I was told how much you admired it."

"But it cost a fortune." Her voice quavered in a losing battle with tears.

"Did it? I did not notice."

Raoul unfolded the smaller quilt over her lap and she traced the double wedding ring pattern with the tip of her finger. It was beautiful, intricately quilted, and in perfect condition. Her mother had owned three quilts made by Julia's great-grandmother, but following Carleen Parker's death, they'd gotten lost with her father's moves to different army bases.

"The dealer called patchwork an American art form," Raoul murmured. "He said quilts are heirlooms to be passed down through generations, and he hoped these would go to someone who would treasure them always—I told him they would."

Julia sniffed and smiled through her tears. Whether

he knew it or not, Raoul had found the perfect gift. "They're beautiful."

"Gorgeous," Sharon Waterton agreed. She looked at Julia for permission, then spread the large quilt out for everyone to see. The women were enthralled, and even the men looked interested.

By the time the festivities ended, Julia was tired, but she offered to help clean up the usual mess of paper plates and spilled punch.

"Absolutely not," Maggie scolded. She was directing activities in her own quiet fashion and soon had a work party organized, including package bearers to help load Julia's car.

"If you will allow me," Raoul said, when he walked Julia to the parking garage. "I will follow you home and carry these things into the house."

Julia nodded and sighed gratefully. Her back was aching again, and she had a secret longing for the kind of foot massage Raoul used to give her in Washington.

It was so muddled. She wanted to be strong. She knew that she could only really depend on herself, and yet Raoul was proving her wrong. Heck, he was doing his best to be supportive and noncontrolling, though it had to be killing him not to insist she do things his way.

At the house she curled up on the couch, and before he'd brought the second load inside from her car, she was sound asleep.

Raoul lifted the antique quilt rack from the trunk of his Mercedes and carried it into Julia's bedroom. He'd decided not to present it at the baby shower, fearing she would decide he hadn't been "discreet" by publicly giving too much.

But there was no longer any need for secrecy, and warmth crept around his heart at the memory of her announcement. He only wished she'd also announced they were getting married.

Muppet, Julia's jealous cat, regarded him suspiciously from his position on the back of the couch. His mouth opened in a soundless hiss.

Raoul tucked a blanket around Julia as she slept, then fixed Muppet with a stern eye. "You will not touch my daughter, is that clear?"

The feline blinked.

"I have dealt with tougher cats than you, my friend. You are no match for two-hundred pounds of Sumatran tiger."

Muppet calmly extended his hind leg and licked behind it, displaying an insouciant lack of concern for threats. Raoul chuckled. He would become friends with this Muppet eventually. They both adored the same woman, how could they not be friends?

Adored...

Yes.

He adored Julia—for her fire, her warmth, her tender heart. He had never felt so much love for a woman, and she had taught him to care equally for the daughter sheltered in her womb. Carefully, trying not to disturb her, Raoul sat on the floor and cupped the precious mound. He was afraid for his child, and for what would happen to Julia if things did not go well. Her heart would shatter, more surely than crystal striking rock. And he was utterly helpless to do anything but watch.

The house was dark when Julia stirred and yawned. A slight weight lay on her lower abdomen, and she looked down, astonished to see Raoul asleep, his arm extended over her stomach.

He looked uncomfortable, as though he'd fallen asleep while he was just sitting there, touching her.

The thought sent heat to her cheeks, though she knew he wouldn't have touched her intimately—not when she was asleep and could not agree or object. Raoul Oman had a number of faults, but that wasn't one of them.

Julia slid her fingers through his thick black hair. It was like coarse silk. She'd loved doing that when they were together in Washington. Loved the feel of him as he kissed her, held her, devoured her. She closed her eyes again and drifted with sensual memories. Raoul was an experienced, adventurous lover, without any inhibitions. In the bedroom, at least.

What was it he'd said?

That she'd been the one in control in Washington, not the other way around? Julia turned on her side and rubbed the strained angle of his shoulder. There were different kinds of control. Maybe he meant the kind where if she said no, then no was the end. Or maybe she just couldn't recognize the give and take of a healthy relationship, never having had one before. If things were ever going to work out sharing the parenting of their daughter, she'd have to learn to compromise a little better.

"Chère?" Raoul muttered sleepily.

"How did you know it was me? Or *did* you know?"

"I knew." He lifted his head and stretched, working out the tension in his upper body. "There is no one like you. Your scent, your warmth. You have spoiled me for other women."

"Lucky you, landing a job in Chicago where I happened to live."

Raoul turned on a light and gazed down at Julia incredulously. "I am far wealthier than Kane Haley, and responsible for managing my country's financial affairs. Do you really think I require a job?"

"I guess not."

He waited, then sighed. "The truth is, I wanted to continue our affair. Looking back, I am not proud of my reasons, since you had made it clear you wished an end to the relationship, but it turned out for the best."

She sat up and swung her feet to the floor. "You mean, considering that I'd lied."

He sat on the low table next to the couch and caught her shoulders in his hands. "No more guilt, Julia. I am excited about this child. I want to be a good father and know I can only do it with your help."

"You're the one who grew up with a good father, Raoul. I hardly think I'm qualified to teach you anything about parenting."

"No? You have so much love for the baby. Is that not the one thing that you missed most in your childhood? Is that not what you want most for our daughter?"

She nodded, and he dropped a kiss on her lips.

"We agree, then. Now…shall we practice our Lamaze? As you said at the party, I do want to get my hands on you."

Whether he'd said it to break the tension, or to flirt, it succeeded. Julia laughed and climbed to her feet. "I'll get the pillows. Why don't you call and order some Chinese food."

"Do you have a particular craving?"

Julia thought about sweet and sour chicken and her mouth watered. "Yes, sweet and sour chicken with extra sauce. And anything with snow peas…as long it's all peas and they're still crunchy. And fried rice," she said over her shoulder.

The light was on in the bedroom and Julia stood for a moment, looking at the quilt rack sitting by her bed. Raoul must have brought it in while she slept. It was perfect to display the antique quilts he'd given her.

Raoul didn't make a fuss of his wealth. He'd only explained about the money so she'd understand it was no coincidence or accident that he'd come to Chicago. It wasn't a declaration of love, but she'd never had a single other soul who'd tried so hard to give her what she wanted and needed. She went back to the living room, pillows clutched to her chest, looking solemn.

"Thank you," she said.

Raoul looked up and shook his head. "For what?"

"The quilt rack…everything. She's going to be one spoiled baby." It was easier to pretend he'd done it for the baby, but she knew better.

"That is nothing. You should see the diamond tiara I'm getting her."

Julia laughed and threw a pillow at him.

They settled down, Raoul holding her from behind, his hands stroking her swollen stomach as she focused and tried to pretend she was really in labor. She'd shied away from thinking about the delivery, mostly because she'd expected to be alone. The doctor had said for some women it was similar to cramps from their period, just more intense, and since she'd had pretty terrible periods, she could believe it.

"You're not focusing," Raoul breathed in her ear.

"I know you want always to be in control, but can't we be partners in this?"

Control.

There was that word again.

"Remember what the instructor said?" he continued. "A woman's body knows how to give birth. I will follow your lead, but we should work together to make it easiest."

"Right."

She focused again, counting and breathing. It was strange their instructor hadn't talked that much about trust, at least when it came to the Lamaze coach. A woman had to trust her body, as well as the person supporting her through labor, and all the practice in the world wouldn't make a difference without it.

Julia wasn't sure how much she trusted herself, but she was pretty sure she trusted Raoul.

When the doorbell rang she frowned, wishing they could just go on practicing. She'd even forgotten the discomfort of sitting on the floor.

"I think that's our dinner," Raoul murmured.

Her eyes flew open. "Answer it quick, I'm starving."

His low chuckle rumbled through her, and he rose. "I hope they remembered the snow peas. I offered a big bonus for what you asked."

She smiled, put her arms back for support, and stretched out her legs. She'd never seen someone who enjoyed spoiling another person the way Raoul spoiled her. And, though she had niggling questions about the kind of woman who let herself be spoiled, she was going to savor every bite of her snow peas.

"Excuse me, I may not have the right house. I'm looking for Julia Parker. I'm her brother."

Oh, God.

If she'd had any clue her brother was going to show up, she *would* have moved out of state. As if in slow motion, Julia watched Raoul step to one side, letting Lieutenant Lyle Parker step inside.

Lyle wasn't stupid. His gaze zeroed in on her swollen stomach, then her bare ring finger, and he actually glared. He swung around to face Raoul. "Who the hell are you?"

"Not that it's any of your business, but he's Sheik Raoul Oman. And don't you dare talk to him that way," Julia snapped furiously. Raoul deserved respect, a lot more than Lieutenant Lyle Parker.

"I'll talk any way I damn well please."

"No, you won't," Raoul warned. He rocked forward on the balls of his feet. "Be careful what you say, and how you say it."

"Are you married to her?"

"My relationship with Julia is none of your concern."

Lyle drew himself up into a smug, self-righteous posture. "It's my concern if she got herself knocked up without a husband. For the last time, are you married, Julia?"

She crossed her arms over her tummy. "No."

"Do you know what this is going to do to Dad?" he exploded. "The people in Washington won't like hearing their new four-star general has an unmarried pregnant daughter. It doesn't look good. Damn it, Julia, you know we have to follow higher standards. How could you get in such a mess?"

"So he finally got that fourth star," she said, not particularly worried what the Pentagon thought of her decision to have a baby. If they had a problem with it, they could come talk to her. Besides, she doubted it was all that important to anyone but Lyle and her father.

Her brother swore, low and in great detail, the kind of foul language he'd learned on various naval bases.

"Be silent," Raoul growled dangerously, looking for all the world like an enraged tiger protecting his mate.

Lyle turned and without a blink, took a swing at him.

"Stop," she shrieked. Her brother was a Navy Seal, he could kill with his bare hands and a thousand other ways besides.

Everything happened in slow motion.

One minute Lyle was lunging with a thirst for battle, the next minute he was lying on the floor, nursing a dislocated shoulder and even more dislocated pride.

"I told you to be careful," Raoul said. "It is a shame they didn't teach manners when they made you an officer. You wouldn't make a decent private in my country."

Lyle's face was stunned. He obviously didn't know what had hit him.

Raoul actually winked at Julia. "I thought you said he was sudden death in every direction," he said.

"Guess I was wrong." An unholy glee filled her. If a man had ever deserved comeuppance, it was her brother. Deep down he was a decent guy, but it was *way* deep down.

"Mr. Parker, I suggest you leave, and do not return unless invited," Raoul said. "I'll call a cab if you are unable to drive."

"It's all right, I have to deal with him sometime," Julia muttered.

"He's leaving."

"Raoul."

"I will not allow him to upset you, nor will I tolerate him speaking to you without respect."

Julia was torn. She'd always dealt with her brother's boorishness and her father's insensitivity on her own, and Raoul was being his usual high-handed self by ordering Lyle out of the house. On the other hand, no one had ever defended her quite so fiercely. It both annoyed and touched her.

She struggled to her feet, ignoring Raoul's attempts to help. She looked at his set face, then at her brother, and sighed.

"You heard him, Lyle. Get out and don't come back unless you're invited."

Chapter Ten

The food arrived the same time as Lyle's taxi, and Julia carried it to the kitchen while her brother left—presumably to go to the hospital to nurse his war wounds.

A *civilian* hospital.

He wouldn't want anyone to know he'd been taken down by a man who was an inch shorter, twenty pounds lighter and had no navy training that he knew of. And, while Raoul had successfully dealt with Lyle, she was still shaking inside. What if he'd missed or slipped or something?

"Are you angry with me, *chère?*"

"Yes. You could have gotten blood all over my carpet. Broken that antique table. Put holes in the walls."

Raoul smiled. He was learning about Julia, and thought she might be hiding her concern beneath a curt exterior. "My father insisted each of his sons serve a tour with our army. Men like your brother forget that size is not always the deciding factor in a confrontation."

"Yeah, well, he was always willing to take me on."

Raoul's smile faded and he put his hand over Julia's. "I should have taken him outside when he lost control. I frightened you, which is the last thing I wanted. Do you need to see the doctor?"

"What? No." She shook her head. "I have my regular appointment tomorrow, anyway. What I really want is my dinner."

They ate from the cartons, Julia keeping her gaze fixed to the food as she munched on crisp snow peas and fried rice and drank milk. But it wasn't long before her shoulders began shaking and tears welled from her eyes. He'd known it was coming, and in an instant had her close in his arms.

"It's just hormones," she sobbed into his shoulder.

"I know, *chère*, I know." And he rubbed her back while she cried. She wept for a long time, and he knew it was a necessary release. Things had gotten too tense, and he'd handled it badly.

"He could have killed you," she whispered finally, her breaths still coming in ragged shudders. "He really could have killed you."

"No one will hurt you, Julia, or keep me from seeing my daughter. Please believe me, I've been well-trained and was never in any danger. I think your brother talks bigger than he can perform."

All at once Julia sat up straight on his lap and scrubbed her cheeks with a napkin. "It *is* hormones," she repeated with grave dignity. "I'm not one of those women who cry during commercials and because I broke a fingernail."

"Tears do not make you weak."

"You want me to cry because I broke a fingernail?"

Raoul chuckled and kissed her chin. "Probably not.

Are you certain you're all right?'' he asked putting his hand on her stomach.

"Fine, just tired.''

Without a word he lifted her and carried her to the bedroom.

''I could have walked.''

''Allow me to do this small thing.''

Julia lay back against a pillow and let Raoul pull the comforter over her. She'd have to change into a nightgown later, but for the moment she could stay put. Turning onto one side, she watched him build a fire in the fireplace and turn out the light.

It was nice to feel cherished, and she let herself wish for a single weak moment that Raoul loved her. Her feelings for him were so confused, though she tried not to think about it. Maybe letting someone support you through the hard times didn't mean you were weak, maybe it was a partnership, the way Raoul said.

Sharing the good and bad...it sounded nice. But there was still the question of whether she could have more children, and whether a royal son of Hasan could truly give up sons for an American wife.

Julia sighed and closed her eyes, too tired to worry about it tonight. She could sleep in her dress. It was wrinkled anyway from her nap on the couch, so what difference did it make?

At her appointment the next afternoon, Dr. Svenson was thoroughly amused at the story Raoul was telling. He was one of the old brand of doctors, the kind that believed in warm concern and getting to know his patients.

''Julia, did you actually say 'so he finally got that fourth star?' And nothing else?''

She shrugged. With Raoul's easy charm, he'd made the whole thing sound comical, while at the same time ensuring that the doctor knew she'd had an upset the night before.

"My brother is a pain in the behind. But Rambo, here, took care of denting his dignity."

"Rambo?" Raoul asked, puzzled.

Julia and the doctor laughed.

"Rambo is a film icon in America," she explained. "All fists and muscles and big guns."

"Ah."

Their fingers were laced together while she lay on the examining table. Without making it obvious, Dr. Svenson was being more thorough than ever checking her—and he was pretty thorough at the most ordinary of times. Strangely, she didn't feel self-conscious about Raoul being there during the exam, and she had a sneaking wish that he'd been there during all the other ones, as well.

"You can get up now, Julia. Everything is fine," the doctor assured her. "You're going to have a lovely little girl in a few weeks."

The two men went out, still talking, while Julia dressed and thought about wanting things she couldn't have, and wondered why she wanted them.

It was a question that zinged around her head the next few days with unrelenting intensity. When they weren't working, Raoul seemed to spend more time at her house than at his hotel, and he was unfailingly patient with her growing crankiness. Julia wanted to blame her pregnancy and the quicksilver hormones it churned up for her bad moods, but it was mostly the unsettled state of her emotions.

He hadn't said anything about wanting to get married since her last refusal. And she was pretty sure she'd accept if he asked again, because she was pretty sure she loved him. At least she'd seriously think about accepting.

On the next Thursday she sat at her desk making notes on a pad of paper, when she felt the first sharp pain.

"No." Julia dropped the pen and clutched her stomach. She had almost three weeks before her due date and the baby needed every one of those weeks to gain weight. Taking deep breaths, she tried not to overreact. Maybe it was nothing, her body adjusting to a rapidly growing baby, or it could be Braxton Hicks contractions. They said false contractions could feel quite real.

Everything in her abdomen seemed to be shifting, and she grabbed the phone. She wanted Raoul. For the first time in her life she had perfect clarity, no questions, he was the one person who could hold her together.

"Be there," she prayed, dialing the number.

It rang three times, and she was panicking when he finally picked up. "Yes?"

"R-Raoul?"

"I'll be right there."

In his office Raoul dropped the phone and shot out of his chair, terrified by the tone he'd heard in Julia's voice. He raced past others in the hallways, turned the corner and burst through the door. He paused for an instant, taking in the chalky white of her face and the way she held an arm over her abdomen.

He swallowed, willing himself to be calm. If she needed anything from him, it was cool, clear thinking.

"I think…I'd like to go to the hospital," she whispered. "I'm not sure, but it feels…." All at once she drew a harsh breath and tensed, a contraction rippling visibly across her swollen belly. "Oh, God. She's too small."

He knelt by her, stroking the hair from her face, damp now with cold perspiration. "It will be all right, *bien-aimée*. We'll call the ambulance, just to be safe."

Julia nodded, one short bob of her head. He eased the telephone receiver from her clenched fingers and dialed the emergency number, then the obstetrician's office. They assured him the doctor would meet them at the hospital.

Some of their co-workers were gathering at the door, asking questions and generally making noise. He sent them a warning look. Uneasily, they shifted backward, quiet falling on the group.

A moment later Kane pushed through and crouched on the other side of Julia. "Security just called, the ambulance attendants are on their way up," he said softly.

Raoul nodded, his attention centered on the woman he loved more than life. The fear he felt for his child was nothing compared to the terror of losing Julia. And he felt an impotent fury at the way nature had dealt its hand. A woman's body was made to bear children. She'd done everything right, damn it. Why couldn't this *one* thing have happened the way it should?

A stir outside told him the ambulance attendants had arrived and he slipped his hands under Julia, lifting her in his arms. She was rigid with fear and he kissed her forehead.

"If Muppet is jealous of me, imagine how he'll feel when we bring our daughter home," he said. "He may decide he has to move to another country."

It was a poor joke, but Julia smiled, some of her stiff tension easing. "He's starting to accept you."

"Yes, he only hissed *twice* last night." Raoul put her down on the stretcher, only to have her grab his hand, refusing to let him go.

Kane asked everyone to go back to their offices, told them that he would keep them posted...that it was probably nothing. Anxious onlookers drifted away, giving Julia privacy while the attendants checked her out.

"Don't worry, ma'am, your vital signs are good," the leader assured. "Is this your husband?" he asked, looking at Raoul.

"He's the baby's father. I want him to stay with me," Julia said, her grip tightening on Raoul's hand.

"I am not going anywhere, *chère*," he murmured. "They could not order me away."

"Bet I could," she retorted, with some of her usual sassiness, and he smiled.

"Ah, but would I listen?"

"Probably not."

Julia had only one more contraction on the drive to the hospital, and she was starting to feel hopeful when a burst of warm liquid between her legs made her gasp.

"Raoul!"

"Shhh," he soothed, his watchful gaze noting the dampness spreading on the blanket covering her. "We are nearly there."

Dr. Svenson was waiting at the ambulance bay, and, though his eyes had a hint of concern in them, he greeted her cheerfully. "Jumped the gun, did we, Julia?"

"'Fraid so."

"Well, now, that isn't so bad." He patted her shoulder, the image of a kindly country doctor. "The baby should be plenty big enough. You'll both be fine."

Without seeming to hurry, he got them through admitting and into a room in record time. Julia looked around after his examination. There was a bassinet along one wall and she remembered this particular hospital allowed babies to stay with their mothers.

That is, if the baby was healthy enough.

She shivered, cold again, until Raoul sat next to her on the bed. He kissed the inside of her wrist, and she knew he was hiding his own worry to keep her calm.

"What…what if the doctor was wrong? Weight estimates from ultrasounds aren't always accurate," Julia said. "She might be smaller than he thought."

"Or larger."

"Y-yes." The thought was comforting, though not nearly as comforting as the gentle massage he was giving her abdomen.

"We haven't discussed baby names," Raoul murmured, his fingers continuing to move in the same easy circles. "Did you have one in mind?"

She did, but she'd meant it as a surprise. Of course, now was as good a time as any for a surprise. "I thought, if it was all right with you and the rest of your family—Rihanna Carleen, after both our mothers."

Emotion, warm and powerful, exploded in Raoul's heart and he bent to kiss Julia. "I would be honored," he breathed into her lips. "And my mother will adore it. She has so longed for a granddaughter."

"Ye-sss." The word came out as a sibilant hiss as another contraction overtook her. The hours of Lamaze training and practice clicked into place, and Raoul spoke softly, rubbing her stomach, helping her concentrate and ride through the pain.

In the first few hours everything was fuzzy to Julia, clouded by worry. She followed Raoul's voice like a lifeline…it coaxed, cajoled and ordered her when necessary. He wouldn't let her give in to the panic, and she gradually pushed it into the back of her mind.

In a quiet moment he called his parents. It was the middle of the night in Hasan, but they asked to speak with her—saying nothing much, yet reassuring her just the same. Afterward, she cried and asked Raoul what they'd think if they knew the truth about their affair. He just kissed her and said it would make no difference.

Once in the delivery room, Julia's thoughts cleared, her mind focused on giving birth. She hadn't really believed the Lamaze instructor, but she *did* know what to do. It was Raoul's voice, his urging and the demands of her body that she listened to, not the doctor.

The pressure eased once the baby's head and shoulders were delivered, and a moment later the infant was out entirely.

Before Julia had time to ask if she was all right, an angry little shriek split the air.

It's cold out here, that voice seemed to be saying, and a watery smile filled Julia's face. Dr. Svenson put the baby on her stomach so she could see and touch her miracle.

"She's fine. Perfect," the doctor exclaimed, his face grinning broadly behind his white hospital mask. "And I think she's a few ounces over five pounds."

"Darling...oh, sweetheart," Julia quavered, her fingers cupping the baby's head. "Don't cry, Rihanna, we're here." She looked up at Raoul, who was watching them both, tears falling unnoticed from his eyes.

As her body prepared for the last stage, delivering the placenta, Dr. Svenson wrapped the baby in a flannel blanket and handed her to Raoul.

"Hold her, Dad. Mom and I have more work to do."

Raoul stared down at his tiny daughter in awe. She was the most beautiful thing he'd ever seen, next to her mother. She had his dark hair, and eyes he hoped would be hazel-gold like Julia's. She wiggled and stopped crying and made funny movements with her mouth. He could scarcely believe he'd helped make something so perfect.

He remembered to encourage Julia to focus one more time, and heard the doctor's pleased remark that she was doing well, with no abnormal bleeding. A gratitude such as Raoul had never felt before swept through him.

This was it.

The key to everything.

These two females were the loves of his life, and whatever it took, he wouldn't let them go.

While they were still in the delivery room, smiling nurses took the baby and weighed her, gave her a warm bath, then put her to Julia's breast. In wonder, he watched his daughter nuzzle, then latch onto a nipple and begin to suckle. Julia drew a swift breath, tensed and relaxed.

"That's it," encouraged the head obstetrics nurse. "She knows what she wants. Nothing shy about that little one."

"Can we have her in my room?" Julia asked eagerly. "She's big enough, isn't she?"

"She sure is," Dr. Svenson said. "Five pounds, four ounces. You did a good job, young lady."

"Thank you...thanks for everything."

He patted her shoulder, a suspicious moisture in his eyes. "They're taking you back to your room now, I'll be in to check you both later."

Julia's eyelids drifted closed as the adrenaline faded.

She was barely aware of being moved, only knowing the sweet warmth of her baby, and the soothing stroke of Raoul's hand on her hair.

When Julia woke late that evening, she was sore, though not as much as she'd expected. The hospital had tried to make their obstetric rooms as homelike as possible. Nice curtains hung at the windows, peaceful paintings of meadows hung on the wall, and a Mother Goose lamp sat on a table, its light softly illuminating the room.

Next to the bed was a comfortable, oversized chair where Raoul sat, his attention focused on the baby he held. Rihanna Carleen looked extraordinarily small in comparison to her tall daddy.

"You are so little, *mon tresór*," he was murmuring. "I am almost afraid to touch you."

Rihanna let out a funny little yelp, and Julia's body responded, her breasts tingling, her abdomen tightening. She wanted to try nursing again, yet she was reluctant to disturb father and daughter.

"Hey, there," she said finally, and Raoul looked up. "Have you been holding her this whole time?"

"Yes."

"So you're spoiling her already?"

He looked down at the baby again with a silly, wonderful smile. "She doesn't seem to mind."

"No." The baby made a sweet gurgling sound, and Julia couldn't wait any longer. "Um, I think I need her."

She shifted in the bed while Raoul put the baby on her stomach and helped adjust her gown. She ought to have felt awkward, but there was something natural about the moment, and he stroked the small baby's hand while Julia tried to get Rihanna interested in her breast.

It didn't take long.

The suckling sent curious sensations through Julia—some of it not so comfortable because it triggered a contraction of her uterus—but mostly it was breathtaking.

"Do you know how perfect you are?" Raoul asked in a low voice, and she looked up from the baby. He sat next to her, his gaze so warm she nearly melted.

"I'm not perfect. Far from it."

"You are to me. I love you, Julia."

"Don't—" Her voice choked. It was what she wanted to hear more than anything, but she needed it to be real. "You should give yourself some time to sort things out. Rihanna and I aren't going anywhere, and it's overwhelming, seeing your baby born. You might be misunderstanding what you feel."

His eyebrow shot upward, but it no longer annoyed her, because it was so much a part of him. "You think I have been overcome by sentimentality?"

"Not exactly, but—"

Raoul put his hand over Julia's mouth, stopping whatever it was she wanted to say. *Mon Dieu,* how he adored this woman. She was protecting him, even now. But he did not need protection, he needed her.

"I knew that I loved you more than a week ago," he whispered. "Knew that I had fallen in love with you in Washington and never stopped. I hid it from you, from myself, concealed it with talk of physical need and desire. But Julia, you are my one true mate. I could never be happy again if we were apart. We don't have to live in Hasan, we can live here in Chicago...anything you wish."

"Raoul," Julia said raggedly.

"Just tell me you love me, *ma chèrie*. Please tell me."

"I do, but—"

"No more buts." Happiness filled his face, more joy than she'd ever seen.

"Don't you understand?" she asked desperately. "Don't you remember what I said? I might not be able to have more children. You might never have a son."

Raoul shook his head. "If we do not have a son together, then I will never have one, regardless. There could be no one else after you. And I am content with our beautiful daughter—she is more than I ever dreamed of."

"Your parents..."

He shook his head. "They want me to be happy. My mother knew immediately that you were my destiny— told me I would regret losing you for the rest of my life. She has annoyed me many times with her match-making, but this time she was right. I might be slow to know the way of my heart, but I'm not fool enough to lose you."

"I—"

A sudden commotion in the outside corridor made Julia hastily pull a blanket over both her breasts and Rihanna. A gigantic teddy bear appeared in the door's opening, so large it concealed the bearer.

"My name is Edward," a gruff voice said. The bear's arm waved as if saying hello. "I'm looking for a new friend."

Julia's eyes widened.

"Daddy?"

Raoul made a low growling noise, but didn't say anything.

"Yes, it's me." The bear moved to one side, and she saw her father's lined face, looking older than his years. He was dressed in full dress uniform, with every one of his medals and decorations pinned to his chest.

"What are you doing here?" She knew she didn't sound welcoming, but this was a special day and she didn't want him ruining it.

"I..." General Parker cleared his throat. "Lyle called and told me about your pregnancy."

"I can imagine." Hard as she tried, Julia couldn't keep the bitter edge from her tone. What she didn't understand was why her father would bring the baby a teddy bear when he surely agreed with Lyle that she'd made a mistake and embarrassed his illustrious career.

General Parker put the bear down in a corner chair, then stood awkwardly, not seeming to know what to do with his hands. "Lyle expected me to be outraged, but I was pleased." His voice got really rough again, and he coughed.

She blinked. "Why?"

"Because I was afraid you'd always be alone, like your brother and I have been. When I heard about the baby, I knew you wouldn't be...and that it might mean we could start over." He looked at her, and for the first time in her life, Julia saw tears in her father's eyes. "I did badly raising you. I didn't know what to do with a girl without her mother, and I thought if I didn't make you tough, you wouldn't survive."

"You don't know your daughter," Raoul said harshly. "She is stronger than you can ever imagine."

"I know."

"Do you?" Raoul demanded, as always, charging to her defense. "Do you have a clue how magnificent she is?"

Julia smiled, happiness washing through her. Her father couldn't ruin anything, and it was good and right for the man she loved to defend her. She wasn't sure she would have gotten through everything without Raoul, but it didn't make her weak. If it took two people to make a baby, then relying on someone else when things were hard must be the way God meant it to be.

"I know." General Parker said again, a speculative look on his face. "Are you my grandchild's father?"

"Yes." Raoul looked at him narrowly, his posture aggressively protective.

"That's right," Julia said, deciding she needed to contribute *something* to the moment. "Raoul is the baby's father. And if you'd leave for a little while, I could propose to him in peace."

Raoul spun and stared at her. "Propose?"

She gave him a smile and adjusted their sleeping daughter on her shoulder, pulling the blankets around to keep her modesty intact. "It's only fair, you proposed the first time."

His delight grew and grew. "I accept."

"I haven't actually proposed yet."

"Yes, but I'm not giving you a chance to change your mind."

Neither of them noticed Ward Parker tactfully depart, closing the door behind him.

"All right, will you marry me?" Julia asked, discovering how easy it was to propose when you've already been accepted.

Raoul sat next to her, filling his eyes with the radiance in his beloved's face.

"With all my heart," he promised, and leaned down to kiss her.

Epilogue

Julia carried a pitcher of lemonade onto the deck and put it on the table. Raoul was down on the lawn, bouncing three-and-a-half-year-old Rihanna up and down on his stomach while she screamed happily and begged him to make her go higher.

"That child is fearless," said Jamal Oman. He was watching his only granddaughter with a fierce pride.

"She takes after her father," Julia agreed.

"And her mother," the elder Rihanna added. She squeezed Julia's hand and urged her to sit down. "You are doing too much. You mustn't get too tired, child."

Julia smiled and obeyed. After all these years, she had a mother again. Raoul shared his family generously. They were loving, exasperating, interfering and absolutely wonderful.

A lot had happened since Rihanna's birth. Julia doubted she'd ever be comfortable with her brother, but her father had become increasingly close. It wasn't easy for General Ward Parker to express his feelings, but she finally knew his gruff exterior hid a man who loved her deeply.

Julia poured lemonade for everyone and took a swallow from her own glass, grateful for the cold liquid on such a hot day. She'd hated leaving her old house, but they'd found a wonderful place overlooking the lake, and on sultry Chicago afternoons it caught a cooling breeze from the water.

"Here comes the princess," Raoul declared, coming up the stairs with his daughter perched on his shoulders. He gave Julia a lingering kiss, then lowered Rihanna into her lap.

"Having fun, dear?" Julia asked her daughter.

Rihanna smiled sunnily and Julia smoothed her dark curls. She was a remarkably good-natured child, full of energy and interest in the world around her—and so bright it was a challenge to keep up with her quick mind and nimble fingers. After a minute she climbed down and ran to her grandfather Jamal for a hug.

Raoul pulled Julia's feet into his own lap and began massaging them. She squirmed lower in her chair, prepared for a delicious few minutes, when a loud squall came from the baby monitor on the table.

"I'll go," Raoul said, but she shook her head.

Nevertheless, he followed her inside. With his arm looped around her waist, they went into the twins' nursery and saw Ward standing in his crib, his lip curled unhappily.

"What is it, little man?" Julia murmured. She kissed his warm cheek and checked his diaper. He needed changing, and she deftly replaced it with a dry one.

Raoul watched his wife and son and knew a moment of such perfect happiness it threatened his composure. The twins were recovering from chicken pox, and he marveled at Julia's loving patience for each cranky cry and petulant pout.

Ward took his medicine and got a bottle of cool water, and then it was his brother's turn for attention. Khalil was less demanding than Ward, but his mother always ensured he was equally petted and adored.

As she did their father.

Dr. Svenson had warned him she would need to focus so much attention on the twins that he might feel neglected, but it had never happened. Julia was one of those rare women who made everyone in her life feel they were the most important person in the world.

"They'll probably fall asleep again if we leave them alone," Julia said as they tiptoed from the nursery. "The antihistamine makes them sleepy."

"Yes, I am sleepy too."

"You are?"

Raoul grinned and kissed her neck. "I think a nap sounds very...desirable."

"Your parents are here," Julia reminded, but she didn't sound too interested in stopping his roving fingers. "And my father is coming later."

His hands settled on her hips, pulling her bottom against his aching groin. "Then we had better hurry."

She giggled. "As I recall, that's how I got into my current state. Being in a hurry."

"Mmm, yes." He skimmed his palms over her still-slim waist, and then higher, cupping the sweet warmth of her breasts. "Who knew you were fertile as a turtle, *bien-aimée?*"

Her laugh was so filled with contentment he rejoiced again. "I don't think it's all me," she said.

He'd worked her into their own bedroom, and he kicked the door closed behind them.

"Oh, it's you, *tresór*."

With a smile that said he couldn't wait much longer, he stripped her clothing away and had her on the bed in seconds.

"Only you do this to me," Raoul breathed, rubbing his hardness against the soft warmth he needed so badly. He gathered her lush breasts in his fingers and kissed the pebbled nipples, flicking his tongue and teasing her, resisting the urgent thrust of her hips.

"That does it, I'm taking over." Julia pushed his shoulders and he obliged by flipping over on his back. He grinned, wondering why he'd ever wanted a compliant woman in bed, especially when Julia rose above him and, ever so slowly, threw her leg over his, smiling naughtily.

"Whatever you want, my dearest love. The mother of the possible future queen of Hasan deserves the greatest respect and obedience."

Julia froze. "What are you talking about?"

"Rihanna. She *is* the eldest grandchild, and if my brother Malik doesn't marry, the royal line falls to us."

"No way." Julia's bare bottom landed on his stomach. It was delightful, but another part of his anatomy desired her attention more. "Hasan may be as advanced as you told me, but even Great Britain isn't ready for direct female succession, not if there's a younger boy in line."

"Yes, I suppose you are right. Of course, that leaves the eldest grandson..." His voice trailed suggestively.

"That means...oh, *you*," Julia hit him lightly with her fist. "Ward is *not* going to rule, you monster."

"As you wish, Princess Julia."

"Don't call me that."

"But you *are* a princess. Her Serene Highness, the Beloved Princess Julia Oman of Hasan."

"You don't have to rub it in. If I'd known about that Serene Highness stuff I probably wouldn't have married you."

Ah, he loved to tease his democratic American about her royal title. She might feel uncomfortable being royalty in his country, but his people did not feel the same. They adored their new princess and eagerly looked forward to each of her visits. Her official portrait hung in most homes and shops, and by popular demand she'd been honored on Hasanian stamps and money.

"You would have married me," he said confidently. "You are far too intelligent to keep passing up such a fine husband."

"That's true."

"And I don't think we have to worry about our children securing the royal line. I have it on good authority that Malik is considering marriage. It seems he is impressed with the happiness his sister-in-law has given his brother and wishes to experience it himself."

"That's nice." Julia pinkened a shade at the compliment. "Um—you don't want our children to be in the succession, do you, Raoul?"

"Absolutely *not*," he said, so forcefully she couldn't doubt it. "I want to live in Chicago with my wife and go sledding with my children in the winter."

Julia moved her palms over her husband's smooth chest, giving him a sensual massage. "Don't you miss living in Hasan?"

His hands eased her backward. "I only miss being inside you, my darling wife. So if you would be so kind…?"

She took him in, and after a few moments he turned

over with her, thrusting hard and fast. Before she had time to think, she felt her body shatter into a thousand pieces, only to be gathered back again by the velvet voice whispering in her ear.

Afterward, she lay cuddled next to Raoul, her thigh nestled between his. Her second pregnancy had gone like a textbook case of childbearing. She'd delivered the twins with a short, and thank goodness, not early labor. They'd weighed seven pounds two ounces and six pounds fifteen ounces, respectively—good-sized babies compared to their older sister.

So far her third pregnancy was going equally well. Kane Haley had approved her working at home part of the time, so she was able to be with the children and still be active professionally. Raoul continued as Chief Financial Officer of Kane Haley, Inc., advising Hasan's new Minister of Finance as needed. The day might come when they needed to spend more time in his country, but for the present they would continue living in Chicago.

In the moments when they lay quietly together, Julia often wondered at the path they'd taken. Raoul said he wouldn't change their courtship, except for the problems she'd had carrying Rihanna. He was sincere, believing they wouldn't be together if fate hadn't placed them in each other's path. She teased, claiming it had been more like a collision course, but she'd come to peace with her deception. The thought of being without him was too unbearable to waste with regret and questions.

Each day Raoul showed his happiness in a thousand different ways. They still argued, but making up was sweeter for knowing what they might have missed. And she knew that even if she'd never been able to have another child, it would have been all right.

"I love you," she whispered. "Don't ever leave me."

"Never," he promised, kissing her forehead, his strong body sheltering her with all the passion of his love. "Some marriages are measured by years, but ours will live beyond the end of time."

* * * * *

*Turn the page for a sneak preview
of the next*
HAVING THE BOSS'S BABY *title,*
SHE'S HAVING MY BABY!
Kane and Maggie's story!
*By popular author Raye Morgan
on sale February 2002
in Silhouette Romance...*
And don't miss any of the books in the
HAVING THE BOSS'S BABY *series,
only from Silhouette Romance:*

Chapter One

Kane Haley was staring at her with that weird look again. Maggie Steward bit her lip and leaned forward toward her computer monitor so that her crisp navy-blue linen jacket would fall out and hide her stomach. Her heart was thumping. Had her boss guessed she was pregnant?

She went back to typing up the letter he'd asked her to write and wished he would close the door to his wood-paneled office so she couldn't see him sitting in there, staring out at her. And even more important, so *he* couldn't see *her*.

She should have told him by now. She'd meant to. But she just hadn't found the right words. Once he knew she was going to have a baby, she had a feeling things would change drastically—not only professionally, but personally.

Nervously, she pushed a stray strand of golden-blond hair back into the twist at the nape of her neck and tried to concentrate on what she was doing, but thoughts and regrets were straying as well. Once he found out, she had no idea what he might say or do. What if he decided he needed her to transfer to another department so he could begin training someone new?

She valued her job as his administrative assistant, but more than that, she really needed it. The money was much better than for any other position she could qualify for in the company. And finances were turning out to be much tighter than she'd expected. She had no one to depend on but herself. Having a baby cost so much money!

The letter was finished and sliding slowly out of the printer. Ordinarily, she would go right in and have him sign it, but she was hesitating, worried about what he might be thinking. Was he framing the question right now? Was he wondering why she hadn't told him?

Maggie! Get a grip!

She scolded herself and rose from her ergonomically correct chair, being very careful not to move in any way that might emphasize her pregnancy, grabbed the letter and marched right into his office.

"Mr. Haley, if you'll sign this, I'll get it out right away."

"Hmm?" He gazed at her blankly.

As always when her eyes met his, there was a little frisson of excitement that scattered along her nerve endings. Just one of the hazards of working for a man who looked like a cross between a young U.S. Senator and a cowboy—smoothly handsome grace leavened by a core toughness that defined masculinity at its best, as far as she was concerned.

"Oh," he said as he realized what she was there for. Picking up a pen, he held out his other hand for the page. "Sure."

She waited apprehensively for his gaze to make a quick trip down toward her slightly protruding stomach, for his eyes to narrow and his brows to furl, but it didn't happen. He signed the paper, tossed the pen down, and stared into space again, ignoring her completely, his mind obviously captivated by some puzzle that wouldn't let him be.

She frowned, turning her head to see what he was looking at, then turned back again, muffling a sigh of relief. Thank goodness. He hadn't been staring at her at all. He was staring into space, and the space he was staring into just happened to be in her direction. He hadn't noticed a thing. Her heart lightened.

Still, something about all this staring did bother her. This was not good, and it wasn't like him. His mind wasn't on his work. She'd been noticing that more and more often lately. What was going on?

Walking back toward her desk, she carefully closed the door to his office, then went over possibilities of disaster as she slid into her seat. What if he was thinking of taking another job? What if he was bored and wanted to start a new business in some other place? What if he was about to quit his position and sail around the world on a catamaran? He'd talked about doing that once—gone on and on about the romance of the high seas.

She didn't want him to go anywhere. Not only would she lose her job, she would lose…him. Her cheeks reddened. She had to stop thinking about him like that. After all, their relationship was totally work-related. But a little part of her wondered if she should make it clear to him that she was free, just in case….

But that was going nowhere. He was a terrific boss. Their relationship was very special to her. She wouldn't do anything to ruin it if she could help it. She only hoped he wasn't planning on anything that would do exactly that.

Of course, her decision to go ahead and have a baby might be enough to put a damper on things. It had all seemed so easy back when she'd begun. Lately, she'd had second thoughts. Not about the baby—but about her timing. Things just weren't falling into place the way she'd hoped.

With a sigh, she went back to work at her computer, resolving to think of a way to tell him she was pregnant.

"Gotta do it today," she promised the empty air. "No more excuses."

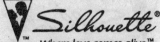

Coming in February 2002 from *Silhouette*

THE
FAMILY
FACTOR

In **BLESSING IN DISGUISE**
by Marie Ferrarella,
a bachelor gets much-needed
lessons in fatherhood.

In **THE BABY FACTOR**
by Carolyn Zane, an assertive
TV producer humbles herself
to get mommy lessons…
from her handsome employee!

Because there's more than one way to have a family…

Available at your favorite retail outlet.

Silhouette®
where love comes alive™

Visit Silhouette at www.eHarlequin.com   BR2TFF

Coming in January 2002 from Silhouette Books...

THE GREAT MONTANA COWBOY AUCTION
by
ANNE McALLISTER

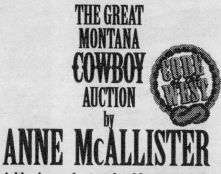

With a neighbor's ranch at stake, Montana-cowboy-turned-Hollywood-heartthrob Sloan Gallagher agreed to take part in the Great Montana Cowboy Auction organized by Polly McMaster. Then, in order to avoid going home with an overly enthusiastic fan, he provided the money so that Polly could buy him and take him home for a weekend of playing house. But Polly had other ideas....

Also in the Code of the West

Available at your favorite retail outlet.

Silhouette®

Where love comes alive™

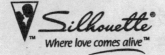